COCKTALES

VOLUME ONE

A collection of eight erotic stories

Edited by Miranda Forbes

Published by Xcite Books Ltd – 2012
ISBN 9781908766427

Printed and bound by CPI Group (UK) Ltd, Croydon, CR0 4YY

Cover design by Sarah Davies

Contents

The Deepest Dig
by Sylvia Lowry

I had uncovered the last quarter of the mosaic, careful to avoid damaging the fragile coloured tiles, delicately applying my brush to remove the desert sands. Before me, resplendent, lay a preserved image of a woman, arched and ecstatic, her nude figure open to the universe. In that moment, I envied her as I admired the figure, her eyes gazing towards the heavens, exquisitely rendered in flakes of antique stone. Watching the skies above me, working in the oppressive heat of the Egyptian afternoon, I felt a different, less emboldened kind of exposure, the defencelessness of a vulnerable mortal. I could feel the sweat pour down my back as I took another drink from my canteen, stopping for a moment to catch my breath.

In my career as an archaeologist, I had always felt ambivalent about exposing the past. There is a nakedness to the artefacts of history, a profound frailty, and perhaps I had exposed this new figure against her will. Whenever I uncovered a fresco, a jar or a relic of daily life, I had always imagined that their figurative nudity became mine. The hard precision of scholarship became something more rousing and intimate.

And in examining this new figure, I experienced an undeniable thrill, a pleasure in the act of uncovering, a subversive feeling that reminded me of the ecstasy of a sexual encounter, delicious in its brief passing. As I took a momentary break from the dig, I realised that I had become literally exposed; in my final battle with the dust of the tomb, my breasts and nipples were revealed by the sweaty dampness of my T-shirt. For a moment, the desert air caressed them, forcing me to shudder with brief arousal, as if the spirits of the tombs had conspired to banish my solitude.

Then I saw Clive, digging near the closest rock formation. I waved and saluted, and he responded with an innocent shout of 'Deeper, deeper!' as his pick invaded the soil. I smiled at the mild innuendo. We had only spoken occasionally as we worked together, but he had fascinated me since the first day of the excavation. I would hesitate to call my fixation a schoolgirl crush, but my infatuation had a youthful, innocent intensity. I didn't need to know a man well to have an erotic fascination; perhaps it was easier to want to fuck a colleague than befriend him.

'Be gentle!' I teasingly shouted back and resumed my work, but the initial uncovering of the mosaic had drained my energies. I used my finest brush to dust off the mosaic, as if I were sparing her from the further aggression of my pick. The sun had mercifully begun to descend, and I idly admired the nude form again, struck by the delicacy of its workmanship, the details of the face that seemed to radiate personality and pleasure. But then the light of the sky faded, and I realised that the workday had ended. At the camp below the site, I could see that Clive had begun to cook dinner.

I felt hesitant to return to camp, but I finally summoned the courage to descend the path, imagining myself as the woman in the mosaic, charged with sexual allure, brazen and heroic. But my confidence vanished as I approached

Clive, who sternly faced the fire. A half-full mess kit drifted into the sand beside him.

'Eating baked beans while I do the housework?' I laughed and seated myself, reaching for a glass of wine, consuming it fretfully.

'Anne! Did you finish the mosaic?' His eyes opened wider, as if he were astonished by my dedication. In the wake of my fatigue, I quickly calculated our achievements for the day and imagined that he had done little to equal my dedication. And as I surveyed his ass, highlighted by the flush of the fire, I felt a different kind of fervour, imagining myself reaching towards him impulsively, kissing him gently before accelerating my attentions, unzipping his trousers and silently taking his cock in my mouth. Yet I remained silent, mired in my inhibitions.

'Yes.' I nodded, feeling a brief flush of wine. 'I uncovered all of the surface of the figure, or what appears to be all of it. I'll need to study it by daylight. There might be more to uncover.' I hesitated and gazed at the fire. 'You can join me, if you'd like.'

He nodded wearily. 'Only if I have time. I need to finish reviewing the pottery samples by noon.' He completed his meal and gazed into the darkness. 'I could sleep like a Pharaoh, honestly.'

'You're going to bed? I wanted to discuss the strata of the outcrop.' I laughed after I spoke the phrase, which I had spoken with mild irony. I wanted to ensnare him with my words and allure, to ravish him by the declining flames, to shred his clothes like a wild carnivore and wrap my pussy around his cock, and as I watched him depart, I finished my wine in a defiant swallow, wanting to cast the glass into the fire, cursing my timidity. I could see him disappear into darkness, a fine escaped quarry, and I allowed the flames to die, permitting the darkness to enfold me and obscure my presence, imagining myself vanishing into a comforting void. My nagging reflections returned: I had sacrificed the comforts of a conventional life in the name of scholarship and lamented that I had not been fucked in over two years. I lamented my unsatisfied appetites, watching the expanse of sand stretching into infinity. It reminded me of my figurative carnal desert, bleak and unrelieved.

Returning to my tent, I fell asleep almost immediately and dreamt that I was lying on an ancient bower, nude and reclining in the posture of the woman in the mosaic, legs spread defiantly to the world. I first placed two fingers in my pussy, luxuriating in the friction of a substitute cock, twisting my nipples as I lurched my ass skywards, imploring the ancient gods to reward me with an energetic fuck. And as I pumped my fingers inside my cunt, feeling a fraction of release that only reminded me of an absent cock, I dreamt of a tongue forging a delicious trail along the inside of my thigh. As it paused to lick the inside of my legs, offering generous attentions to the crevasses behind my knees, I imagined I saw Clive materialise, gazing into my eyes, his mouth ascending to my pussy, where he inserted his tongue without ceremony. I leant back and let him invade me, licking to an unfathomable depth before sucking my clit, salivating generously, allowing the delectable spittle to cascade along my cunt. I ran my fingers through his hair, clutching his tresses in desperate fistfuls as I started to come and moan an invocation to the skies ...

And as the orgasm ripped through my pussy, ascending through my nipples and throat, my reverie was interrupted as I awoke to the sound of footsteps and the shadow of a passing silhouette. Rising from my sleeping bag, I saw

Clive walk by as if he had been incarnated into flesh by the sheer force of my imagination. I sat up, tired and alone as I watched him seat himself on an outcropping, staring into the darkness. I quickly dressed and approached him, only modestly covering my nudity.

'Anne?' He spoke quietly, seemingly surprised at my arrival, returning his head to his knees.

I approached further. 'Would you prefer to be alone?'

'No, not at all.' He spoke in a neutral tone, the pitch verging on melancholy, tapping a compass insistently. 'I need something to complement this wretched instrument. I think I messed up my coordinates earlier. I could swear that it was pointing towards Cairo an hour ago.'

I laughed meekly. 'The mysteries of attraction, I suppose? Or do all roads lead to Cairo?'

In the desert night I imagined I heard a remote shriek, its source unidentifiable, shuddering across the rising dunes. Maybe he was contemplating an unrequited passion of his own. But his thoughts were unobtainable. His head leant towards the sand, his mind descending, I imagined, into the depths of some distant excavation site.

I put my hand on his arm. 'The question sounds ridiculous, but do you ever imagine that you can expose your entire self?'

He looked towards me. 'Figuratively, you mean? Exposing your inner being?'

I paused. 'Maybe. I was thinking about the mosaic of the woman that I uncovered. I realised that I'm the only one who's seen it in its entirety for a millennium. Or what I imagine is whole – there could be more – but I'm fascinated by the pose. It appears complete, but I imagine there's something below, waiting for discovery.' I looked towards him, but glanced away. 'I feel like there are so many things like it, just waiting for expression.'

He laughed. 'I'm not sure I understand.'

I smiled, moving closer. 'I can demonstrate.'

'Demonstrate?' His eyes expressed a charming eagerness laced with terror.

'Let's stop talking about work ... and start to play.' I moved my hand to the back of his neck, first applying gentle pressure as I stroked the fine hairs, leaning forward as I whispered into his ear, gently laughing inwardly at my bravado. Licking his inner ear, deviously plumbing the entrance with my tongue, I murmured, 'There's something else I want to uncover ... your exquisite cock.' He started briefly and I pulled him towards me, imagining him ensnared as I reached towards his crotch, sensing his energies emerging, caressing the contours of his shaft through the fabric. 'And you're not going to fucking resist.' I could feel new moisture in my panties as I savoured the charged moment, kissing his cheek gently, then his lips, my fingers eagerly seeking his entire cock as it shifted beneath the fabric, ascending into a full and rigid erection.

He lay backwards onto the sand, and I envisioned an ancient statue settling into rest. He remained passive, nearly inert and I smiled impishly as I unzipped him, gazing into his eyes as I removed his cock from his trousers. I touched it gently and admiringly, as if it were a new archaeological discovery. Perhaps it was. How long had it been since I had touched one? My professorial eye admired its details: the neatly shaved scrotum, tensed with arousal; the exquisite shaft, quivering with anxious delight; the striking, engorged veins pumping with warm blood, and the inflamed head, silently inviting me to lick and suck with unrestrained ferocity.

But then my carnal instincts resumed, and I let a mischievous drop of spittle descend. As it struck the engorged head and glazed the side, I licked it up with a deliciously sloppy motion, murmuring in undisguised pleasure. I retreated onto the sand, seated on my knees. 'You taste fucking fabulous. I've been waiting weeks to suck you off.'

He glanced upwards, exhausted by the shuddering climax. 'My God, Anne. Why didn't you earlier ...' I smiled as his wounded thought trailed into the darkness and resumed my attentions, gripping the base of the shaft, enthusiastically jacking him off as I savoured his cock with enthusiasm, startled by the intensity of my rising, wanton appetites. My inhibitions had vanished suddenly as I began my enraptured blowjob, and my ravenous energies now inspired me to play with my inflamed clit as I allowed his delectable shaft to caress my tongue. I salivated generously along its length; there was something nearly culinary in the delightful sensation.

I licked his balls waywardly, and could have continued. But then I could sense a throbbing pulse as his balls tightened, the unmistakable crescendo of a rising orgasm.

'God, Anne ...' He threw his head backwards with a fevered, oddly endearing intensity.

'No worries, baby.' I kissed the head of his cock, savouring its uncontrollable pulsation. 'We can fuck later. Come in my mouth, man.' I was delighted by my powers of suggestion – as if on command, a volcanic, sloppy fusillade of come jettisoned into my lips and I savoured the incoming barrage like a gourmand, murmuring with contentment, surrendering to the filthy pleasures of the moment.

I hugged him fraternally and we resumed our observation of the night, which had begun a subtle transformation into dawn. A blushing finger of pink light crept incrementally across the plain, eclipsing the darkness as I hugged him more tightly, awakening to an increasing sensation of comfort and warmth, sensing the illumination, now traversing the camp, strike my half-exposed breasts. I opened my shirt further, emboldened by my disclosure to the awakening morning, enjoying the lingering taste of Clive's luscious come.

It was a foretaste of victory, but I wasn't through with him yet.

I grasped his arm. 'Let's go to the tomb.'

He laughed. 'So early? I thought we could continue ...' He gently kissed my cheek as I stood up and gestured emphatically.

'First, I have a theory about the mosaic.'

'A sudden epiphany?'

I did not answer, but grasped his hand and led him to the path. We climbed towards the burial site, now illuminated by an emergent column of sunlight, the mosaic of the woman awakening in my mind, her ripe breasts and exposed nude form enshrined in time. Below her magnificent ass stood a layer of encrusted sediment. Its opacity tempted me – I was compelled to dig further, to increase the scope of my earlier revelation.

I leant towards Clive, kissing him gently on the lips. 'Let's dig. Carefully.' Jointly, we brushed away the soil of the ages, respectfully liberating the image below. New contours began to take form, colours emerging in resplendence as the sunlight mounted in intensity, casting a spotlight on the startling image: the woman sat atop, or rather mounted, a second figure, the unmistakable form of a sexual partner, supine on the ancient wall, his erect cock penetrating his liberated partner in reverse cowgirl position. Her ecstatic expression burned even brighter in my mind, and I imagined her thoughts lost to the vibrant friction of an unashamed fuck, enshrined in eternal rapture, naked to infinity.

'Here.' I placed my hand on Clive's shoulder, fixing my gaze into his eyes as I removed my shirt, casting it onto the sand, lying backwards in invitation as I removed my trousers and discarded them into a neighbouring dune, unabashed and naked with the exception of my panties, which I pulled upwards into my moist pussy as I teased my clit through the sheer fabric. I relished the delicious friction of the cloth against my sodden cunt, gazing upon the mosaic, imagining myself boundless and free. I moved the garment to the side to place a finger inside myself, dramatically spreading the cloth like a curtain's revelation, masturbating as I smiled at Clive.

'Get down here and fuck me with your tongue.' I licked my lips and grasped his hair, propelling his face towards my glistening pussy, delighting in the abrasion of his stubble against the inside of my thighs as his tongue invaded me, plumbing the inside of my cunt, plunging inwards momentarily before he lapped at my clit like a beast. I pinched my nipples, pulling them towards the heavens, feeling my areolae warmed by the arriving sun. I ripped off my panties and reached towards his cock, sensing new vitality as the shaft hardened, the head pulsing with the arrival of enthusiastic new blood. As if he had sympathetically obeyed my desires, he removed his shirt and trousers, discarding them into the sand as I grasped his erection and guided it inside me, leaning backwards as its length caressed my lubricated depths. He first began slow, tentative strokes before he fully marshalled his confidence, licking my neck in playful, gentle contrast to the ferocity of his thrusts. I grasped his ass, caressing his balls in wordless encouragement, lurching upwards to kiss his nipples and neck.

He thrust his cock into me maniacally, fucking with mechanical intensity, as if he had also been possessed with the spirit of the mosaic, and I surrendered to the insistent friction of his cock while I slapped my clit. My pussy was now literally soaked, inspired by my rising fervour, and I could feel my juices cascading delectably around his shaft. But I was inspired further by the image behind us.

'I want to get on top – I want to fuck you like she's doing it.' He lay back passively as I seized his shaft, driving it inside myself with such sudden intensity that I could hear him gasp in surprise as I mounted him in reverse cowgirl, a perfect reflection of the ancient image.

All propriety vanished, the world evaporated, as we entered a primeval world of shifting sands, regressing into a realm of total exposure. I watched the mosaic as we fucked, united in liberated candour with the ancient image, all pretensions of scholarship cast to the sands. There is something about riding a cock, the sense of gentle domination that it provides, the ability to control the angle, to stimulate the clit. And as I nailed him, I imagined that I silently commanded him, communicating beyond language. He bucked rapidly upwards to meet my thrusts, as if he had read my filthy imagination.

Finally, I uttered, 'Fuck me from behind; I want to feel your balls slapping my fucking ass,' and he complied without hesitation as I turned over, my nipples uniting with the earth as his cock plunged back into my pussy, his hands gently grasping my waist as he screwed me with mounting zeal, increasing the depth of his barrage. I imagined, fancifully, his cock emerging from my throat as a shiver rose through my pussy, then through my nipples and the tendons of my neck, inspiring an animal utterance or perhaps an ancient hieroglyphic expression of primal release. I came, kicking my legs in elation as he withdrew, ejaculating in a ferocious eruption across my ass, followed by second and third bursts of semen, scattering with diminishing force across the small of my back.

I looked back towards Clive, facing the emerging sun, extending my arms in an embrace of its pagan energies, gazing towards the encampment, unashamed. I caressed my breasts and nipples, embracing my nudity as the woman in the mosaic gazed back, unearthed and enlightened, boldly enraptured in her perpetual fuck. I devoured her energies, turning back to Clive, caressing his balls as I played with my clit, inviting him to fuck me into eternity.

Heat It Up
by Shashauna P Thomas

When it comes to what turns people on sexually, everyone has their own kinks. Things that are guaranteed to rev them up from zero to 90 in seconds. For some it's the sight of leather bondage and handcuffs, while others love pedicures in high-heeled shoes. Everyone has fetishes whether they want to admit it or not. I bet if more people were open with their sexual hot buttons they'd find their fetishes are more common than they think. Take mine for example. I love a man in uniform. For me there's always been something hot and rugged about a man dressed up in the standardised uniform of their profession that seems to make them even more appealing. Almost like the generic uniform tries to cage their innate masculinity and emphasises them instead. Mailmen, bus drivers, officers, doctors, surgeons, and paramedics all get my feminine juices flowing. However, my reaction to all of them combined is nothing compared to what happens when I see a man in what I consider the definitive panty soakers ... the fireman uniform.

It doesn't matter if they're suited up in hard hats with matching yellow and black jumpers or if they're wearing the plain dark pants, light short sleeve shirt or dark coloured T-shirt with the fire department initials on the back. Either way I want to lick them from head to toe. Grab one by his suspenders, hop on him, wrap my legs around his waist, and proceed to play tonsil hockey for a few hours. I love firemen. One of the first things that I noticed about my apartment when I first moved in was that it was directly across the street from a firehouse. The noise of the area in addition to the noise of the fire engines was one of the reasons the apartment was so affordable. Others might not like living so close to a firehouse, but I personally consider it a perk.

Looking out the window every day and getting glimpses of the strong, muscle-bound men was slowly driving me insane. Watching them wash down the engine, pile into the engine while racing off to respond to a call or just hanging around the firehouse often had me sitting at my bedroom window salivating like a starving dog with a bowl full of bones directly just out of reach. I hadn't even met them yet and they were affecting my sanity along with my libido. It was pure insanity that spurred me into action. With a tin full of homemade chocolate chip cookies I made my way across the street to the firehouse. I had no idea how myself or my cookies would be received, as it was the first time I'd ever been inside a firehouse. I had no idea if they had any rules about civilians being around but I figured there was only one way to find out.

Lucky for me the bunch of guys I first met were extremely friendly and welcoming to a young attractive woman walking right in with a bunch of cookies. It just so happened that the first one I walked into was the chief. He was a nice older man who, off the bat, made me feel welcomed and reminded me of my father. The chief said he didn't mind me coming around as long as I promised not to get in the way when a call came in. All the guys were nice, friendly and, in general, good guys to hang around with. I started coming at different times to meet the other guys who worked different shifts. Some were hot and some were average but in their uniforms, none were disappointing.

I enjoyed hanging out at the firehouse with the guys. They enjoyed my company as much as they enjoyed my cooking skills. I found out that the guys took turns cooking, and some were better at it than others, so my little contributions to the menu were always welcomed. Even the chief enjoyed my cooking while teasing me that I was trying to fatten them up. I'd make them cookies, brownies, fried chicken, meatloaf, and a number of other things. I came so often I knew each and every one who worked there. Who was married, who had a girlfriend, who was single, who had kids, who didn't, who was a comedian, and who was serious. Mark was the serious one.

Mark was the strong silent type. He was always polite, and didn't say much to me, but the way I'd catch him looking at me when I was in the firehouse told a totally different story. In regards to size, Mark was the biggest firemen there in height and muscles. I knew he was intelligent from the short talks we managed to have but mostly from conversations he had with others that I overheard. Mark had been a fire-fighter longer than most in the station and, from what I've gathered, had seen more fires then the rest of them. When he'd strut around the station that experience exuded in everything he did along with restrained power that seemed to roll off him in waves. Even with his massive size he reminded me of a graceful lion prowling his territory. He was the physical embodiment of every single fireman fantasy I'd ever had. It didn't matter that I knew him the least out of all the firemen; I knew I wanted him and no one else would do. My only problem was how to get my hands on him.

Lucky for me, an opportunity unexpectedly presented itself.

It had been a really busy week at work. I barely made it home for a quick nap, shower, and a change of clothes most nights, much less had the time to cook something and bring it over to the boys in the firehouse. That Friday night I had just enough energy to make a pan of lasagna before I collapsed in the bed from exhaustion. Saturday night I had planned a much deserved evening out with the girls so I woke up early Saturday afternoon and treated myself to a spa day. I spent the whole day pampering myself. With my hair and nails done, wearing the new outfit I'd bought, I was more than ready for a number of drinks combined with an evening of dancing and flirting with friends at a club. On my way out I grabbed the lasagna deciding to drop it off at the station on my way out. It was summer so I wasn't cold in the short black skirt, tank top, and heels. As usual, the big bay doors were open, the lights were on, and one of the engines was parked half in and half out. The only thing out of the ordinary was how quiet it seemed inside. Even though I'd been coming there for months I still hadn't had a tour so I had no idea where everyone was. The only sounds I heard were the clicking of my heels on the pavement and a TV on low. I figured it was coming from the small lounge I'd seen off from the dining room.

As I leaned against the cracked door I said, 'Hello?' The only light in the room was coming from the glowing television, illuminating the lone figure sitting on the coach facing away from the door. It was still too dark to see who it was, but I could see he had turned around and was now facing me in the open doorway. 'Hey, where is everyone?'

'Oh hey. A couple of the guys went out shopping for

groceries. The rest are sleeping upstairs.' The deep timbre of the voice told me who it was before he reached over to the lamp on the side table. With the dim lighting I now saw Mark standing in front of the couch facing me with a can of soda in his hand. His button down uniform shirt undone, exposing the white wife-beater underneath cascading over rippling abs.

'I didn't think you guys ever slept.' I replied, well practised in hiding the butterflies in my stomach that he never failed to provoke. 'I just stopped by to say hello and to bring you boys some of my lasagna.' He didn't respond, just stood there staring at me with his dark intense eyes. He's always quiet but I'd never seen such an intense look from him before. It was making me more nervous by the minute. 'Should I just leave it on the table or should I put it in the fridge?'

'You can leave it on the table. I'm sure when the guys get back they'll want some. That is if the guys upstairs don't finish it off first.' He replied with a smirk. I nodded and made my way next door to the eating area. This part of the firehouse I was well familiar with. After placing the tin in the middle of the table I turned around and almost jumped to find Mark leaning in the doorway watching me. I hadn't expected him to follow me, and he was so silent I hadn't heard him. 'Do you usually make lasagna dressed like that?' It was then that I realised this was the first time he'd seen me dressed up. I usually came to the firehouse dressed casual. No wonder the fire I normally see in his eyes seemed to be raging tonight.

Shaking my head no, I replied, 'Not exactly. I'd been so busy I really hadn't had the time to bring you guys any of my cooking so I made a lasagna last night. Thought I'd come by, visit for a while, and drop it off on my way out for the night.'

16

'Well as you can see everyone's either asleep or not here ...' He said as he strolled into the room closing in on me and my personal space. '... but you could visit with me for a while if you're interested.' His voice getting deeper by the moment.

'I think I can manage to spare a few moments.' Smiling deviously as I brushed past him and on my way out of the eating area and back to the main bay. Stopping in front of the huge red fire-truck an idea began to form. So I turned around to face Mark as he closed in on me once again. 'You know, of all the times I've been here I still haven't received the grand tour. How about you give me my own private tour starting with the engine?'

'Sure.' He replied and proceeded to show me around the fire-truck. He took his time pointing to different parts of the truck explaining what they were called and their function. It was interesting and any other time I would've been spellbound and asking ten million questions but the subtle little touches he managed to casually slip in kept distracting me. The feel of his hands on my exposed skin frazzled my brain and nodding my head seemed to be all I could manage.

Then glancing up at the front of the fire-truck behind the cab, I managed to ask, 'Can we see the inside?'

'You sure you can get up there in those heels?' Mark chuckled.

'You'd be surprised what I'm capable of doing in these heels.'

'Pleasantly surprised no doubt.' He replied as he helped me up onto the silver steps into the truck by conveniently placing his hands on my thighs and he easily lifted me up to the first step. I knew the inside of the truck would be cramped with a low ceiling, but once one sits down on the dark bench seating you can see that there is enough headroom as well as enough space for a number of firemen to fit when responding to a call. We sat on opposite sides facing each other as he continued to explain what everything was. Leaning back with his arm up in the open window slot, his eyes continued to blaze with interest as they roamed up and down my body. When he finally ran out of things to explain I decided to take advantage of the quiet and finally make my move. With my stomach fluttering I knew it was now or never.

'I know you're attracted to me, Mark, as I am to you. So tell me why this is the most time we've spent together and why this is the first time you seem ready to give me the time of day?' I asked in a sulky voice as I slowly began running my hands along my body.

'It was for your own good. You're a small petite little thing, and I'm a big guy who likes to get really rough with my partners. I still don't know if you're able to handle me, but you make it incredibly hard to deny what I want to do to you.' He reached down and adjusted his pants making room for the enormous erection begging for attention.

'Oh I've just begun to make it hard for you, Mark. Why don't you let me worry about what I can and can't handle while you worry about making sure you satisfy my needs.' Slowly spreading my legs wide enough for him to see up my skirt as my hand slowly inched up the inside of my leg. I began rubbing myself through my black thong; moaning as I imagined it was his big hands that were playing between my legs. Slipping two fingers under the thong rubbing my juices into my engorged clit. The only sounds were my elevated breathing and my hand moving in my moisture.

'Show me what you like, baby. Use your other hand to play with your nipple.' Keeping in mind that at any moment one of the guys sleeping upstairs could come down, I tried to keep my moans as low as possible. Lifting my hand I pulled my fitted tank up exposing my bare breast to his eyes. Mark sat there across from me with his hands balled into tight fists as I masturbated for him. The look on his face, the tension radiating throughout his body, and the lust burning in his eyes had me so turned on I felt my orgasm beginning to build a lot sooner than expected. 'That's it, baby. Come for me. Let me see you come apart.' His voice was all I needed to push me over the edge. I bit my bottom lip muffling the sound of my release. I was still trying to get my breathing under control when he said in a deep commanding voice 'Come over here.'

Standing on shaking legs and hunching over slightly I walked the few steps to stand directly in front of him. With one hand he took mine and began to suck the juices off my fingers while the other reached under my skirt. With a strong grip on my thong he tugged hard, ripping it off me. He leaned forward and roughly consumed my nipples. Alternating between sucking and biting. His hands massaging my butt as mine held his shoulders were the only things keeping me upright; my legs felt like jelly. Suddenly he released my breast and flipped me around before pulling me down onto his lap. Spreading my legs open so I straddled his thighs. He played with my nipples as I began grinding on his dick through his pants. I couldn't remember a time I'd ever been so aroused. The man drove me insane, and the only thing that would've been hotter was if he were wearing his yellow jumpsuit and hard hat. Oh the things I'd imagined doing to him with those suspenders.

'Undo my pants.' Even though his voice was a whisper in my ear I heard the command in his voice.

19

Causing me to shiver as I reached between our legs and undid his zipper. Somehow he managed to reach into his pocket and pull out his wallet. Inside his wallet he pulled out a condom then handed it to me then slouched down as he commanded me to put it on. Driving myself crazy as much as him, I took my time rolling it down, paying close attention to the base of his shaft, and letting my fingers graze his balls once the condom was all the way on. 'Oh, you're so going to get it.'

'I'm on fire! I ... I need you to squelch the burning inside. You think you ... you can handle it?' I managed to get out as he rubbed the head of his shaft slowly back and forth over my sensitive clit.

'My pleasure.' He grunted as he positioned his head at my opening and began slowly thrusting. Not stopping until he was fully seated inside me. I began riding him following the pace he set. The feel of him deep inside had me moaning and digging my nails into his arms. His hands continued tweaking my nipples, adding another intense sensation to the numerous others coursing through my body. I felt his mouth nibble at my ear, neck and shoulder. Our slow pace began to increase to a fast and pounding one. His shaft managed to constantly hit my g-spot at just the right angle and I began to moan louder not caring if anyone heard me. Sooner than I imagined I felt my second orgasm begin to build as my inner walls started to contract around him as he pistoned away inside me. Then he squeezed my nipples causing my orgasm to crest. As I came apart on his lap he continued pounding away. Then he managed to get us both down on the floor on our knees, placing my hands on the bench and his on my hips not missing a beat. As my orgasm began to ease, another unexpected orgasm began driving me right back to my peak. I gripped and screamed into the bench seat as my hot fire-fighter grunted as he continued to fuck me from behind, now caught in the throes of his own orgasm. Feeling him come inside the condom and his fingers grip my hips so hard I was sure I'd have imprints later made my third and final orgasm last longer than the others. It was amazing.

By the time we were finished in the fire-truck it was way too late to meet the girls at the bar. I was much too relaxed and sated to go anywhere but home anyway. Luckily we didn't run into any of the others as we exited the truck. I gave him a quick kiss turning to leave. Remembering the lasagna was still cool from the fridge, I said over my shoulder, 'Don't forget to heat it up.'

'I think we already did.' He replied. I heard the smile in his voice and knew he understood what I was referring to just as I knew what he was. To say I slept like a baby that night would be an understatement. I didn't know if we were loud enough to wake anyone up, but at the time I really couldn't care less if they stood in the doorway and watched us. It was so good I still to this day could care less if we were caught and watched. If I was completely honest the thought itself makes me hot all over again. I don't exactly remember what happened to the remains of my thong but I suspect Mark took them. I highly doubt he left them in the truck for the boys to find.

I continued to come by the firehouse to hang as well as bring the boys more of my cooking and no one gave any indication they knew what happened. Mark has been much friendlier towards me and we've hooked up a couple more times since at my place. Each time it seems better than the last, which is hard to fathom as that night in the fire-truck was absolutely incredible. Now that he knows about my uniform fetish he has promised me another private tour of the firehouse. I'm not sure how he's going to manage it without any of the other guys finding out, but I told him as long as he wore his hard hat and suspenders, I was game for anything. I really do love a man in uniform and enjoy doing my part to support the local fire department.

Just Watch Me
by Justine Elyot

Until last year, I hated having my photograph taken. In my graduation picture I have fringe in my eyes and I'm hugging a bag to my chest, as if in defence. Every school group or individual portrait features me looking off, slightly sideways, into the middle distance. Less formal studies taken on family holidays frequently feature the classic forearm-over-face pose. I couldn't even smile for a baby snap.

So my choice of recreational pursuit sometimes brings a wry grin to my face – not in mid-performance, of course, because I'm far too professional for that. But when I'm cleaning up my room, putting away the lube and the toys, or removing my lurid cosmetic veneer with a baby wipe, thoughts of the "funny old world" variety cross my mind. Then I switch off the webcam and log off, and I'm shy Sharleen again.

It was James who brought it out of me. I won't say he put the idea in my head, or changed my personality in some fundamental way, because I have always been an exhibitionist, I think. It's just that the urge was repressed for years and years, and it took some very skilful delving into my buried desires to spring it back out of its psychosexual jail.

James was the first boyfriend to talk dirty to me. I had always assumed that I would hate this kind of sex play, being a prim not-until-the-tenth-date kind of girl back then, but my reaction to his nasty words shocked me deeply. It turned me on! Far from wanting to slide out from beneath him and deal a ladylike slap to his roguish cheek, I just wanted to spread my legs wider, throw my head further back and beg to be told again that I was a bitch in heat who needed cock morning, noon and night.

'You can't get enough, can you, Shar?'

'No, no, more, more.'

'You're going to get more. As much as I can give you. And then I'm going to call my friends and have them come and fuck you too.'

I moaned luxuriously. I knew he wasn't serious, but the *thought* of him seeing me as a girl who would do that was just explosively hot. I imagined myself, taking cock after cock, while his friends (in untucked plaid shirts and two-day stubble) cheered and raised cans of beer to each performer in turn.

The fantasy was broadened and extended every time we fucked, new details being added or experimented with as James worked on discovering exactly what pushed my buttons the hardest and quickest. He was good. Within a few weeks, he had perfected the script, and brought me out of my hiding place and into the golden sun of sexual freedom. I trusted him enough to show him all that I was, even the bits that seemed reprehensible or dangerous, and the high-wire thrill of it kept me buzzing day and night.

'What if we did it for real?' he asked one night, after exhausting energetic sex all over the living room and hallway, with the curtains not completely closed.

'Did *what* for real?' I yawned, examining my knees for carpet burn. Ouch. Yep.

'Had a third party over ... just to watch. Or to ... join in.'

24

My eyes flew wide open. 'I don't know,' I said. 'Are you serious?'

'I just think … it would add something. If it was someone we both knew … and trusted. It could be quite hot. Don't you think? I mean, not if you don't want to, of course!'

'Male or female?'

'Either. Your choice. Both, if you want.' He grinned. 'Or neither. Anyway, it's just a thought.' He sounded agitated now, as if worried that he had gone too far and expected me to run for the hills. 'No biggie. Not a deal breaker or anything.'

'You're a pervert,' I said.

'Well, yeah,' he said, in a "duh!" kind of way.

'But,' I said thoughtfully, laying my head back in his lap, 'so am I.'

In the end, we went for Craig, James' flatmate. He had already heard our extravagant bedroom symphonies and, rather than turn up the sound on the TV to drown out our voices and creaking bedsprings, he apparently liked to put a glass to the wall and listen in. Halfway to voyeur already – he seemed the ideal candidate.

James got me hot and bothered while we waited for Craig to come home from work by telling me about the conversations they had had about me over pints in the local pub. 'He knows what you're like,' James told me, sitting me on his lap and snogging me hard, curtains wide, one hand up my top. 'I've told him that you like it hard and often. I've told him about your sweet, tight cunt and your round, red nipples. I've told him that I've fucked your arse and you loved it. He knows you're a dirty slut and he can't wait to see it for himself.'

'God.' I was gulping, throat dry, knickers soaked. 'Are we really doing this?'

'Relax, babe. If you don't want to do anything, just say the word. He's only going to watch, though.'

His key turned in the lock and I hid in James' resumed kiss, letting him put his hand up my skirt, baring my thigh to the eye of the newcomer, who had thrown his bags down in the hall and was home. Home and hungry.

'Well, well.' His voice was a little unsteady, trying too hard for detached amusement. 'What have we here? James and Shar sitting in a tree K.I.S.S.I.N.G. Please don't mind me – carry on.'

So we did. Carried on clinching on the sofa until my top was off and my skirt down.

'What do you think, Craig?' James broke off from sucking my nipple to throw the question over to the armchair. I looked over at him; he had released his cock and held it in a fierce fist. His face was pink all over, and looked bloated, his eyes reduced to piggy slits of lust.

There were two ways I could go now. I could shake myself out of this madness and bolt from the room, clutching skirt and top. James was a decent sort of bloke – he wouldn't hold it against me. Or I could do what I did – move one of my hands down inside my knickers, holding Craig's eyes all the while, and splay my fingertips across my wet vulva, ready to thrum in a slow, steady kind of way, for the benefit of a stranger.

'You're not shy, are you?' said Craig, trying to keep the tone light, but sounding like a buffoon instead, like the probably-virginal techno-geek that he was. Poor Craig. I felt a little sorry for him. This was strong stuff for an introduction to the thrills of voyeurism. But I was past shame now, past modesty, well past my old-fashioned cast-off morality.

'Actually,' I panted, letting James remove the knickers and bra entirely. 'I am. This seems to be ... an anomaly …'

It came out something like "ammamolomoly" though, because James' tongue had come to land on my clit and I could no longer say long or complicated words.

'Oh my God!' whimpered Craig, crouching down to crotch level for a better view. His spectacle lenses steamed up and I came, for the first time of many, thrusting my hips right at him, right at his face.

He did nothing but watch, that first time. There were subsequent occasions, but he never wanted to join in, and that was fine with me. His bottle-lensed, bug-eyed gaze was good enough for me; enough to take me where I wanted to go.

But Craig got promoted and moved away, and James and I lost our audience. We moved on to dogging, which was interesting, but somehow I could not shake the anxiety that our audience might lose control and harm us, or rob us. I wanted to show myself off in a safe space, it seemed.

Then James came up with what seemed like a perfect solution.

'Webcam,' he said, producing a little metal eye from his coat pocket as we sat in the local pub after work.

'What, like on Skype?'

'Yeah. Except we could do a live streaming website. Or perhaps just make a couple of clips first, until you're confident with live stuff. What do you think?'

'Clips?'

'Yeah. Put them on one of those porny versions of YouTube. See how many people bite. Invite them to come and sign up for a live streaming site. We could even make money from it!'

'I don't want to make money from it. I wouldn't have a clue how to declare it on my tax return.'

'Even better! We'll get loads of punters if they know it's free. Just think, Shar, you could have thousands of men getting off on watching you get fucked – all at the same time. What a head trip!'

'Yes,' I echoed. 'What a head trip.'

Initially, I took some persuading. 'What if I was seen by someone I knew?'

'You can wear a mask, or we can pixellate your face.'

'I want them to see my face when I come, though.'

'Perhaps we can have a Valued Customer programme. The ones who stay on, who we learn we can trust, get to see your face.'

'Maybe.'

'We do it the way you want it, Shar. It's your site. We can be as wild, or as tame, as you like.'

James was in IT, so he knew his way around a few lines of code. He designed a website that was as tackily glamorous as I envisaged, then he got Craig to come down for the weekend and film us on a marathon session, which he cut up into five minute clips and placed on PerveNet.

It was a different kind of thrill, watching my luminous eyes and my grainy body on a snippet of film anyone could watch. The statistics mounted quickly; within a couple of days, thousands of people had watched me spread my legs and make myself come with a vibrator, or seen James fuck me from behind while I hid my face in a pillow. Messages piled up beneath the clips, indicating that there was substantial interest in seeing more of me. 'I WILL PAY TO WATCH U FUCK HER GOOD, DUDE' said sk8rboiNJ, while LetMeWatch69 suggested 'I BET SHE LOVES IT'. Every little comment was like an expulsion of hot breath on my clit; a glimpse into the lust-glazed eyes of an aircraft-hangar full of voyeurs. I imagined them, all standing together, a seething mass of teeth-bared carnality, all focused on my split thighs and open pussy. I liked it.

The site has been live for over two years now, and we have close to 10,000 members. That is 10,000 cocks – and perhaps the odd pussy – being taken in hand along with my thrice-weekly Performance Hour.

I love my work, and I am constantly devising new, fresh and surprising elements to add to all the fantasy staples. Sometimes I go solo, with toys, or just a slow sexy striptease and masturbation scene. More often, James joins in and we will have an enthusiastic, no-holds-barred fuck to camera, watching the comments and messages roll in as we roll all over the bed. Once a month, I do a "request show", where I take a few viewers' favourite fantasies and give them a bespoke re-enactment.

Today's presentation is a completely new spin, though, and I must admit I am nervous. For the first time, I am running a competition. And the first prize is … me.

The competition winner, having been vetted and interviewed by James, but not yet seen by me, is waiting in the living room while I prepare for tonight's eagerly-anticipated broadcast. The idea is that I wrap myself from head to toe in metallic red wrapping paper, finishing off with a huge rosette at my crotch. I look quite fetching, in a strange way, I decide, posing in front of my dresser mirror. I have wound tight strips of the foil-wrapping up each leg and arm and around my torso, sellotaping it in strategic places. Despite the head-to-toe coverage, a person would only have to take hold of the top ribbon at my collarbone and pull for it all to rip in half and fall to the floor.

No mask tonight, or blindfold – the viewing public is made up of our 500 "VoyeurPlus" membership, all of whom have become quite "well known" to us over the course of the site's life, so I need not worry about local boys or stray uncles logging on. I switch on the cam and open for business, shaking with nerves at having to perform the one part of this role that genuinely frightens me – speaking to camera. Usually James does it, but tonight he has a different function, and I must speak the words, trying to sound cheeky and confident while the back of my throat dries and my hands tremble. At least they can't see the blush, as red as my wrapping, suffusing my throat and collarbone beneath the layers of foil paper.

'Good evening, one and all,' I quaver, keeping my body in motion, twirling and flexing, to distract me from the hideous sounds coming out of my mouth. 'As you know, you are here to witness a brand new development on the site – one which we hope will be a success, and can be repeated. Yes, tonight I get fucked by the winner of our recent competition – Mr Pussywatch, as he is known to us, had managed to total the most viewing hours of any member in the past year, so tonight he gets to sample a little bit of what he has seen. Gosh, I'm looking forward to it, and I hope you are too. Remember, keep watching, and it might be you here next time.' I rub the rosette at my crotch, enjoying the rustle, enjoying the thought of all those cocks stiffening to attention despite my nerves.

A few comments are coming in already. 'YOU HAVE A SWEET LITTLE VOICE – YOU SHOULD SPEAK MORE OFTEN'. 'ARE YOU NERVOUS? YOU SOUND NERVOUS.' 'YR HANDS ARE SHAKING – IS YR PUSSY WET YET?'

I turn away from the screen and call down through the half-open bedroom door. 'Are you ready, guys?'

I hear the double footfall on the stairs, and I lay myself down on the bed, ribbon tied, soon to be unwrapped, awaiting my fate.

James enters first, video camera in hand, for he intends to film our scene from several different angles in order to edit a more explicit and interesting film from the crude web footage – hopefully we will be able to sell it. Then, Mr Pussywatch (real name, Steven) slips into the room and I get my first glimpse. He is in his late 20s, with short cropped dirty-blond hair and a grittily attractive face. I have been very lucky, I realise, although part of the perverse thrill for me had been the idea that I might have landed somebody deeply unattractive, or just a bit creepy-looking, like Craig. Steve hooks his thumbs into the belt of his jeans and stares down at me from transparent bluish eyes. He has thick lips and they curl up into a slightly sneery smile.

'Best present I've had all year,' he remarks to James. 'I know what's inside though. Spoils the surprise a bit.'

James chuckles. 'You won't be disappointed, mate. I promise you.' The camera light changes from red to green. Action. 'Go and unwrap her. She's all yours.'

Steven approaches quite slowly, as if he can't quite make up his mind whether I'm real or illusory. When he reaches the side of the bed, he puts out a hand – a large, callused, workman's hand – and lays it on the tight-wrapped slope of a breast. I like the weight of him, and I let myself shimmy slightly, rustling beneath his touch.

'You up for it, Starleen?' he asks. Starleen is my Camgirl name.

'I'm always up for it,' I tell him.

He likes my answer, and kneels down on the bed, laying hands everywhere now, finishing with the big rosette between my thighs.

'I want to see you,' he says. 'And so do the rest of the boys. Let's take this off.' He tucks a finger inside the top

31

ribbon, running from shoulder to shoulder, and jerks sharply downward. The sellotape warps before falling away, allowing the paper to rip with a satisfying sweep from top to bottom, twirls of paper tickling my body and flying across the room. It is the work of avid seconds to bare me from neck to toe, though he seems to want to keep the few strips that vaguely cross my eyes and lips, loosely enough that I can see and talk, but just giving the decorative effect of gagging and blindfolding.

Steve stays on one side of me, conscious of how the camera angle works, presenting my nakedness to the viewers with a sweep of his meaty hands.

'Look at this,' he says, seeming to enjoy his moment of notoriety. 'What a treat. I tell you what, guys; the camera doesn't really do her justice. She is good enough to eat.' He squeezes my tits, watching the nipples pop up above his fists, all hard and cherry red. 'In fact, I might just do that.' His mouth is on the stiff buds, licking and slavering, making sure that the cam picks up the tip of his tongue plastering and coating them. The sensitive nerve endings go wild, sending rapid pulses down to my pussy, causing it to contract and flood with juices. And his hand is there now, discovering the evidence. He pushes one thigh, making sure my lips are split wide and fully visible to my audience. 'Camera doesn't always pick up how wet and juicy she is,' he gasps, lifting his teeth from one nipple to gasp into the unswerving digital eye that watches us. 'But take it from me, she is as fucking wet as … as …' His powers of simile elude him, and he contents himself with pushing broad fingers up inside me, enjoying the sounds and sensations, while he bends his head and devours my tits again. I can feel his erection hard up against my hip now, pushing at the rough denim that restrains it.

32

'Is this good, darlin'?' he wants to know, nuzzling my neck as his fingers spear me. 'I've seen you do yourself so many times ... I can't believe I'm fingering this pussy I've watched three times a week for two years ... and soon I'm going to be fucking it.' He nips my earlobe and I moan. James is crouching down at the foot of the bed, getting an unrestricted view of my spread legs and Steven's thumb rubbing my clit.

'I'm going to come,' I warn them, and James scuttles up to film my ribbony face, mouth open, puffing and blowing, while Steven takes a whole breast in his mouth and keeps the finger-pressure up, up, up until I've committed my orgasm to posterity.

Through blurred, tired eyes, I can see the comments rolling in. 'HOT HOT HOT!' 'WHAT YOU WAITING FOR? FUCK HER!' 'SHE IS LOVING THIS!'

I find myself arse-to-camera, thighs wide, head down while he whips off his clothes. James, to fill the brief time this takes, uses his camera-free hand to stroke and caress my bum, running his hand down my cheeks, then my cleft, to my soaked pussy, just to keep a bit of interest for the audience.

'How are you having her, mate?' he asks Steven conversationally. 'Doggy style always looks good in profile.'

'Yeah, that'll do,' he grunts, bent on action now rather than dialogue. I crawl around to present a side-on aspect, keeping my head low and my bottom high while Steven snaps on a rubber. As he penetrates and fucks me, I imagine – as I always do – what the viewers are seeing. They don't see the headboard, jerking a little with each hard thrust, as I do. They see a hard, thick cock, shiny with my juices, slipping back and forth inside me. They see my stretched lips and his big hands on my hips. They see my shocked face and his determined jaw. They even see James, half-lying on the floor to try and get the most obscene shot he possibly can, pointing his lens up at my filled pussy.

'You are fucking her good,' he says, his voice treacly-thick, the way it is when he is trying to fight lust. He will want his turn soon, I think with a thrill, and I push myself back on Steven's rod, circling my hips, inviting him deeper still.

Steve slams a big palm down on my backside when he comes, which hurts a bit, but at least he is gentleman enough to wait for my own climax before he succumbs to his, which I always appreciate. James catches a close-up of the big red handprint on my rear cheek. 'Oh, I'm going to get a still of *that*,' he crows. 'Screencap of the night, I think.'

I am still recovering from Steven's firm handling of me when James hands the camera over to the competition winner, unzips his trousers and poses me on my knees on the bed for a blow job. I try to catch my breath around his cock, hearing Steve crack open a restorative beer over on the wicker bedroom chair, and wiggle my arse for the camera. What a show they are getting tonight. I feel proud, and urge myself on to deliver the performance of my lifetime, licking my lips and taking James' cock as deep as I can, sucking and squeezing his balls while the corner of my eye strays to the screen.

'DIRTY BITCH – WHY DON'T I KNOW A GIRL LIKE HER?' 'WHEN'S THE NEXT COMP?' 'WHERE IS THE OTHER BLOKE?'

Swiftly, James releases my mouth and spins me round to face the corner where Steve sits with the camera in one hand and his rapidly tumescing cock in the other.

'Fancy another round?' asks my James. 'Come and sit

her on your prick while I put the camera on the tripod. Feel like I have to have her arse, but I can't do it and film it at the same time.'

Steve doesn't need to be told twice; he leaps back on to the bed and manhandles me over his upright cock, plunging me down and clamping an arm around my back so that my breasts press into his chest and my face is snug in the hollow of his shoulder. It feels delicious; rude and satisfying, and the additional element of my open bottom cheeks, expectant of imminent attention, is sinfully piquant. James is soon at our rear, spreading me wide, lubing me up, and then he eases in, talking to camera in his expert way.

'See how I'm gliding in … quite slowly … just filling her up without rushing … and she doesn't even try to resist … cos she loves this … don't you, Star? You love it up the arse … and now you're getting it with a cock in your pussy too … of course, she's had it with a dildo up there before … but never a real-live cock … how do you like it, Star? I think our audience would like to know …'

Our audience will have to interpret my incoherent groans, though, because I am far beyond forming words now. I am Star. I am a star. I am watched, fucked, buggered, brought to my limit and held there, for all to see. I let them take me, both ways, all ways, until my bones give way and I become pure sensation, pure flesh and sex, captured on film for all time.

The first thing I see when I emerge from the fog of multiple orgasms is a gigantic comment rolling across the screen.

'YOU'VE COME A LONG WAY, BABY. KEEP ON COMING! LOVE, CRAIG.'

Two Girls, One Cop
by Elizabeth Coldwell

'Licence and registration, please, ma'am.'

I sighed to myself, watching Janice fumble in her handbag for the necessary documents. This wasn't how the trip was supposed to go. The Nevada desert surrounded us on all sides, reminding us of just how small and insignificant we really were in the grand scheme of things. Ahead of us, the road stretched away to the horizon, shimmering slightly in the afternoon heat. We were supposed to be cruising with the top down and the car stereo blasting out soft-rock driving anthems, not explaining to a traffic patrolman why we were travelling at 22 miles over the speed limit.

'I'm really sorry, officer,' Janice said, giving the man her most sincere smile. 'I completely forgot you only drive at 55 over here.'

The holiday had been her idea, dreamed up the night we watched *Thelma And Louise* together for the first time, her parents safely out of the house and the bottle of Bailey's from their drinks cabinet diminishing at an alarming rate between the two of us. 'That's what I'm going to do on my 30th birthday,' Janice had declared, pouring herself another sticky glass of the creamy liqueur. 'Drive out to the Grand Canyon in a cool old Thunderbird just like that one.'

I forgot about the plan – and her desire to spend a wild

night in bed with a Brad Pitt look-alike – almost immediately, too busy dealing with my vicious, virgin hangover the following morning. Thirty seemed like such a long way away, and Janice was always coming up with fantastic tales of what her future would involve. Yet for some reason she continued to hang on to that particular dream and now, 14 years later, here we were.

The car rental company hadn't been able to supply us with the classic T-Bird Janice had hoped for, but she was happy enough with the cherry red Chevy Camaro convertible they offered as an alternative. It was an eye-catching automobile, and with two blondes dressed in halter tops and tiny denim skirts in the front seats it commanded even more attention. Unfortunately, that attention had come from the Nevada State police.

As the patrolman handed back Janice's licence and the documents the car hire firm had given her, I studied him from behind my sunglasses. A good dozen years older than us, his complexion was tanned and weathered from long exposure to the desert sun, and when he pulled off his small, gold-rimmed sunglasses, his eyes were the palest of greens. His posture suggested he was a man who'd listened to a lot of nonsense in his time on the job, and wasn't prepared to stand for any of it. A man who didn't need to rant and rave to stamp his authority on a situation.

'Well, Miz Butler, seeing as I'm about at the end of my shift, and you're a guest in our wonderful country, I'm going to let you off without a ticket this time. But if I see the two of you again, believe me, I'll deal with you properly.'

'Thanks so much, Officer ...' Janice squinted at the name tag above his breast pocket. 'Ledley. We'll be more careful in future, I promise.'

'You do that, ladies. And have a nice day.'

We sat and waited till he'd got back in his patrol car and driven off before continuing on our way. As Janice steered the convertible back on to the road, she murmured, 'Well, we might have got pulled over by a cop, but at least he was hot.'

I glanced over at Janice, who was grinning from ear to ear. 'That is just so typical of you. We could have been in serious trouble there, and all you're doing is eyeing the bloke up.'

'Come on, Fi, don't tell me that sexy drawl and those come-to-bed eyes did nothing for you. And he wasn't just hot, he was big, too. Those uniform trousers really don't hide much. Just think how it would have felt if he'd had you over the bonnet of the car, giving you a good patting-down. It's worth breaking the speed limit for.'

'Janice Butler, you're just a tart.' Despite myself, I was laughing as I chided her.

'Yeah, and it takes one to know one.'

I gazed out at the passing landscape, not wanting to her to know how close she'd come to reading my mind. There's a submissive streak in me that I usually keep well guarded, but it's guaranteed to respond in the presence of strong authority figures like Officer Ledley. Janice was right; the man was hot, and my mind had taken her line about being frisked by him and was running with it. I pictured him ordering me to assume the position, then running his hands all the way up my widely spread legs. When he reached the tops of my thighs and discovered I wasn't wearing any knickers, my pussy already wet and open from his treatment of me, he'd have no choice but to lift my skirt and spank my bare arse for being such a slut ...

My fantasies grew increasingly inventive as the miles

passed, as I thought of all the uses the patrolman could find for his handcuffs and night stick. I didn't know how much of that equipment he actually carried, but in my mind he had the full armoury and was prepared to use it to enforce his dominance over me.

Janice's voice broke into my reverie. We were approaching the outskirts of a town that was no more than a pinprick on the vast, empty landscape. 'There's a diner just up ahead,' she said. 'I don't know about you, but I could do with using the ladies'. And a cup of coffee would be nice, too.'

'Fine by me,' I replied, and moments later Janice was pulling the convertible to a halt in the car park in front of Della's Diner, alongside a huge 18-wheeler truck. I half thought she might start spinning some tale about being ravished by its driver, but instead she headed straight for the rest rooms while I found an empty booth and started studying the laminated menu card.

A mumsy-looking waitress wandered over, pad in hand. The lines around her eyes deepened as she smiled in greeting. I ordered coffee and a piece of cherry pie à la mode for both of us, suddenly ravenous after a long afternoon's driving.

The coffee was strong and rich; I added sugar and a generous swirl of cream, savouring the taste. By the time Janice joined me, the waitress was bringing over our plates of pie, vanilla ice cream already beginning to melt into the hot pastry.

'Mmm, that looks good,' Janice commented, reaching for her spoon.

For a few minutes we ate in silence, Patsy Cline on the short order cook's crackly transistor radio the only accompaniment to our contented munching. We were scraping the last of the pie from our plates, wondering if it would be too greedy of us to order a second helping, when I heard a familiar voice behind me.

'Didn't I say I didn't want to see you two ladies again?'

I turned guiltily, wondering what we'd done wrong this time. Janice's parking wasn't the greatest, but she couldn't have blocked any of the other drivers in. Then I saw Officer Ledley was chuckling at my confusion, and realised he was joking with us.

'Hi, officer. I thought you were at the end of your shift?' Janice asked.

'That I am, ma'am, but seeing as I live here in Cumberland, and Della's blue plate special is better than anything I could rustle up myself ...'

I was only half-listening. Remembering what Janice had said earlier, I couldn't resist glancing down, in the direction of Officer Ledley's crotch. She was right. He did appear to have something very impressive tucked away in there. The fantasy I'd been enjoying about my dominant patrolman resurfaced, and I murmured, 'So, officer, what did you mean when you said you'd deal with us properly?'

Reckoning that now the man was off-duty all bets were off, I slowly, deliberately, licked ice cream from the back of my spoon, keeping my eyes locked with his strange, pale green ones all the time.

He shifted slightly, as though his uniform trousers had suddenly become uncomfortably tight. 'Well, ma'am, there are ways of enforcing authority in a situation that don't necessarily involve reading you your Miranda rights or filling in paperwork. If the two of you would like to step outside to the car, I'll show you.'

Remarkably, no one in the diner paid the slightest attention as Janice and I left enough money on the table to cover the cost of our meal and give the waitress a decent tip, then followed Officer Ledley outside. Perhaps the sight of two young women leaving a diner in the company of a handsome traffic cop was more common round here than we thought.

Ledley's patrol car was parked in the shade behind the diner, out of sight of the road. Not that I was too worried about being seen; in the time we'd been staring out of the window, enjoying our cherry pie out here in the back end of nowhere, barely a dozen cars had gone by.

Janice and I kept shooting furtive, thrilled glances at each other, sensing something was about to happen that went far beyond any of our previous experiences. Just the fact I was even contemplating the odds of two women to one man, and how such an encounter might play itself out, made me wonder if I'd been infected with Janice's enthusiasm for a truly unforgettable road trip.

'Now, ladies, if this was a real arrest, I'd need to make sure neither of you was carrying a concealed weapon. So, up against the car, please ...'

We got into the requested position, legs spread and palms flat against the window of the patrol car, Janice following my lead. This was so like my fantasy, I could feel my pussy growing wet in anticipation of the moment when Officer Ledley's big, calloused hands would slide up my thighs.

He frisked Janice first, lingering over the curves of her hips and big breasts in a way no genuine arresting officer ever would. I watched, enviously, as his thumbs brushed over her nipples, bringing them to hard points beneath the scarlet fabric of her halter top. By the time he'd patted his way up her legs, hands disappearing under her skirt and doing something I couldn't see but which brought a delighted squeak from her, I was almost groaning aloud in

41

frustration.

'All clean,' Officer Ledley commented, before turning his attention to me. I did my best to stifle a needy whimper as his hands began their exploration of my body, but my reaction hadn't escaped his notice. 'You're a hot little thing, aren't you?' he growled in my ear. 'Bet you'd do pretty much anything I wanted you to, eh?'

'Yes, sir,' I replied meekly. His words went directly to my core, the part of me that thrived on fantasies of submission and control coming to full consciousness.

'So you'd have no objections if I did this ...' As he spoke, he tugged open the neck fastening of my top. The material fell to my waist, baring my tits. While they might not be as generously sized as Janice's, they're sensitive, and the sudden exposure to the cool air, coupled with the excitement of being so efficiently stripped, caused my nipples to harden and press themselves against Officer Ledley's palms.

Officer Ledley caught Janice staring. 'Want me to do the same to you?' he asked. I wasn't surprised that she nodded in response, but I was surprised that instead of undoing her top, he reached round and yanked down the zip at the front of her skirt. When her skirt came down, I saw that, like me, she had chosen to go knickerless, her bare bottom now cheekily on display.

'Top and tail,' Officer Ledley murmured. 'My favourite sight.'

Did that mean he really had done this before? I glanced over my shoulder at him, but he'd put his dark glasses on once more, and his expression was unreadable. The glasses only added to his aura of dominance, and cream trickled from my pussy in response.

'So officer,' Janice purred, 'we've established that Fiona and I don't have anything concealed about our person, but what about you? Looks to me like you've got a very large weapon stashed away there.'

'You're just asking for me to swat that bratty little arse of yours, aren't you?' he replied, but his hands were on his belt, unbuckling it before dealing rapidly with the fly of his trousers. When he brought his cock out, both Janice and I were struck speechless. We'd been expecting something on the large side, but this was a real monster, easily the biggest I'd ever seen, drops of juice already oozing from its circumcised head.

Before we'd even got halfway through admiring it, Officer Ledley ordered, 'On your knees, ladies, and show the respect due an officer of the law.'

It was obvious what he wanted us to do. We eagerly got down, one on each side of him, crouching in the shadow of his patrol car. Janice reached for his thick shaft, her hand struggling to encircle it. As she held it steady, we started to lick. He tasted salty and ripe from his day's work. Janice nuzzled her nose in the crisp hair at the base of his cock, breathing in his distinctly male aroma.

While she went to work on his balls, sucking each of them in turn, I concentrated on his tip, lapping at the sweet spot just below his fat, bulging helmet.

'Any more of that,' he warned us, 'and you'll have me coming before I'm good and ready.' He caught hold of Janice's hand. 'Say, Miz Butler, why don't you take a break and play with your friend's pretty little titties for me? I'm just in the mood to enjoy a show.'

I had no idea how Janice would react to his suggestion. In all the time we'd been friends, we'd never experimented sexually with each other. It wasn't that the idea had never occurred to me, but I'd never seen any evidence that Janice might be interested in girls. Until now, as she eyed my bare tits with obvious relish. As Officer Ledley urged her on, she cupped them in her small, soft hands, pushing them together and circling them with her palms.

'Mmm, that's nice.' I gave myself up to her caress. If our friendly policeman wanted a show, we'd give him one to remember. I kissed Janice full on the mouth, tasting cherries and Officer Ledley's cock. She responded, pressing her pointed little tongue into my mouth. The kiss grew more passionate, our bodies grinding together lewdly.

'Oh, man ...'

We broke the kiss to come up for air and I turned to see Officer Ledley, cock clutched in his fist like a cudgel, stroking himself as he enjoyed our performance. The look of sheer lust on his face, an obvious expression of the effect we were having on him, made me want to be even wilder, even more uninhibited.

'Now, tell me, which of you two ladies likes to lick pussy?' he asked.

'That would be me,' I replied.

'I was rather hoping it would be. Now, Miz Butler, why don't you make yourself comfortable on the back seat of my car, and Miz Fiona can demonstrate her skills for me.'

Like a true gentleman, he opened the car door for Janice. As he'd requested, she sprawled out on the patrol car's broad leather seat, bending her legs back on themselves and splaying her thighs wide, giving me a perfect view of her pouting pussy, shorn of everything but a sweet little heart-shaped tuft of hair on her mound.

I didn't have a great deal of room to manoeuvre, but I arranged myself so I was half in and half out of the car, face nice and close to Janice's pussy.

'I've never done this before, Fi,' she admitted. 'Not with another girl, anyway.' There was a pause as she wriggled on the seat, as though searching for the right words. This was her *Thelma And Louise* moment, her chance to celebrate the enduring nature of our friendship before she went over a metaphorical cliff edge. All she finally came out with was, 'But I'm so glad my first time's going to be with you.'

I smiled, giving her hand a little squeeze. 'Just relax and enjoy, babe.'

Hands pressed against the insides of her thighs, nostrils full of the scent of warm leather and juicy, excited female, I let my tongue sweep over the full expanse of her crease. Starting at her arsehole, I brushed repeatedly up to her clit. She gave a surprised little exclamation of pleasure. Behind me, I was aware of Officer Ledley moving up close to get a better look, but for the moment, this was all about me and Janice.

Broad tongue strokes gave way to rapid, feline licks, concentrating on the area around her clit without ever quite reaching it. She writhed in frustration, arching her pelvis up to my face in the hope I would touch her where she needed it most. Somewhere in the near distance, I heard the hiss of air brakes, and the rumble of a big truck pulling out on to an asphalt road. Briefly, I wondered again about the possibilities of being seen, then decided I simply didn't care.

I was determined to take my time, stringing things out for as long as I could before bringing Janice to orgasm, but Officer Ledley had other ideas. He pushed my skirt up to my waist, then a blunt, short-nailed finger probed at the entrance to my cunt, worming its way inside. A second followed with minimal resistance, then a third. *He's getting me ready for his cock*, I thought, with a shudder of queasy anticipation at being penetrated by something so big.

Beneath me, Janice was oblivious, lost in her own private world of bliss. Inspired by Officer Ledley and his seeming need to be inside me, I slipped a finger into Janice's clutching hole, hooking it upwards to catch the sensitive spot on the front wall. As I licked and rubbed and probed, she squirmed and babbled to herself.

Ledley dragged his fingers out sharply, leaving a void only one thing could fill. Primed as I was, it was still a strain, his cockhead stretching me as wide as I'd ever been. By the time I was as full as I could go, I reckoned there was probably still a third or more of his shaft outside me.

My delighted sigh at having a wet, tight pussy to lick at one end and a freakishly big dick filling me at the other seemed to vibrate through Janice's body, causing her to grab at my ponytail so she could guide me to the very centre of her pleasure. It took us a few moments to find a rhythm that worked for all of us, so that every time Officer Ledley thrust forward, he pushed my face hard into Janice's velvet folds, and when he withdrew I was able to take a breath before plunging in again.

Janice was the first to come, grinding her pubic bone almost painfully hard against the bridge of my nose as her juices gushed out into my mouth. As she flopped back on the seat, spent, Officer Ledley pulled me fully out of the car. I caught hold of the top of the door frame in both hands and hung on for dear life as he pounded into me.

Senses overloaded, held tight in Ledley's muscular embrace, all I could do was surrender to the orgasm that threatened to rip me to shreds. I howled out so loudly I was sure someone would come running out of the diner to see who was in distress.

Ledley pulled his cock out of my cunt, spraying my arse cheeks with a couple of well-aimed squirts of spunk, then it was over. The most crazy, intense fuck of my life, made all the sweeter by having my face buried in my best friend's juicy pussy.

'Well, I guess we should be on our way,' I said, as Officer Ledley zipped up and made himself look respectable once more and I re-tied my halter top. Janice had already recovered her equilibrium, and her skirt, and was combing out her hair with her fingers as she checked her reflection in the driver's mirror.

'Where are you ladies heading?' Officer Ledley asked, as he escorted us back round to our Chevy.

'Oh, we're booking into a hotel in Las Vegas tonight,' Janice informed him.

'Vegas, huh? I've got a friend who works traffic patrol there, likes to enforce the same kind of authority as I do. Officer Stransky. I'll have to pass on your registration number, so she can keep an eye out for you ...'

She? I thought excitedly, waving a final fond goodbye to our uniformed friend. It seemed like this holiday really was about to become the trip of a lifetime.

Making the Most of All in New Zealand
by Eva Hore

I was visiting my cousin in New Zealand. She'd promised me at her wedding if I ever came out they'd take me out and show me the sights. She's married to an extremely good-looking Maori guy, rugged, with chiselled features and a torso rippling with muscles like a body builder's.

The moment I laid eyes on Jeff at their wedding I knew one day I'd have him, so when he offered to take me horseback riding for a bit of sightseeing on my last day there, of course I said yes. My time was running out and I wasn't one to allow an opportunity to slip by, especially when I was feeling so horny after being with them for three whole weeks.

My cousin had to work and she obviously had no idea how I felt about Jeff, even insisting where he take me and what food to pack in the hamper. We waved her off and made our way to the stables to saddle up.

With my thighs spread across the horse's mighty back we galloped along. Jeff had packed a picnic hamper and with the saddle rubbing hard against my pussy I found I was beginning to feel another hunger grow – not for what was inside the hamper, but for what was in his trousers, namely his cock.

We spurred the horses through the sandy edges of an isolated beach, sea spray flying high to refresh me before climbing up a steep embankment. We came upon a secluded area enclosed by dense trees. Grass, thick with fallen leaves, provided a comfortable setting and the pungent aroma of earthiness, combined with the saltiness of the sea, had my senses reeling. The rawness of the environment definitely heightened my desire.

After spreading the blanket out onto the lush grass I lay down upon it and watched Jeff's broad back with an insatiable hunger as his muscles flexed while unpacking the food.

'Looks like you've packed too much,' I said, chewing on a blade of grass.

'You never know how hungry you can get when you're out riding,' he answered. 'Could get thrown from the horse, or it could gallop off and leave you stranded and alone. At least you'd have plenty of food to eat.'

'I'd just find the nearest neighbour, get them to take me back home,' I said smugly.

'But around here there aren't any neighbours. No one for miles around. You can scream until you're hoarse.' He chuckled over the pun on "horse". 'No one would ever hear you.'

'You mean we're all alone out here, totally isolated from the rest of the world?' I asked.

'Yep,' he said. 'Just you and me.'

'Well, at least I've got you to protect and feed me,' I pouted, as sexily as possible.

He eyed me, probably sussing out whether or not I was coming on to him and I was, believe me. I wanted him, wanted to feel his weight on me, wanted to straddle him like I'd done to the horse, feel him inside me. It took all my willpower not to make the first move.

Kneeling beside him, I allowed him to tease me with a strawberry. He placed the fruit just out of reach of my mouth, and as I attempted to bite into it, he pulled back.

This went on for a while, so I lunged toward him, held his wrist tight with both hands, enjoying the feel of a tingle deep inside me as my lips grazed his thick fingers, before biting off some fruit.

Then I too grabbed a strawberry, teasing him as he had done to me, but instead of biting into it, he sucked my fingers, strawberry and all, into his mouth. The laughter died on my lips, only to be replaced by desire, as his tongue teased and licked my fingers seductively. Then, holding my hand steady, he looked deeply into my eyes before biting off a small piece, acting as though nothing untoward had just happened.

'Delicious,' he whispered.

I could feel a blush creeping up my neck as he lay back on the blanket, his eyes narrowing as he stared at me.

'Why don't you eat the rest?' he said.

Flustered, I popped it into my mouth, busying myself by unwrapping the cheeses, chicken, and cold meats that he'd packed and placing them with the fruits on a platter. Dry biscuits, a bottle of chilled Chardonnay, and our lunch was complete.

'To a memorable holiday,' he said, clinking my glass with his after he'd filled them.

'To fulfilling all I desired to accomplish,' I said, looking coyly up at him through my lashes.

'I'll certainly drink to that.' He smirked.

We ate in silence. I was nervous as he scrutinised me, unsure of what else I wanted to say and if I really wanted to make the first move. He was after all, my cousin's husband, but he was also very hot.

He lifted himself up on one arm and again, offered me a strawberry, a large juicy one that dripped down his wrist. As I tried to bite into it he crushed it against my mouth, the pulp smearing over my lips while the juices dribbled down my chin. Like a man dying of thirst, he lapped at my chin, licking off the juice and flesh. It was so erotic and when his tongue snaked its way into my mouth I lost total control.

My hands ran through his hair, over his strong back and down over his arse while his hands pawed at me, crushing my breasts, tugging at my trouser band and plunging in between my open thighs.

Desperate and hungry for sex we tore at each other's clothes, discarding them in a flurry to litter haphazardly about us on the green grass. He smothered my breasts with wet kisses as I lay there, naked before him, my eyes swimming with passion, unable even to focus on the clear blue sky. I held my breath as his kisses moved down lower toward my navel, then over my mound, tickling my hairless pussy as his tongue darted about my slit.

He opened my legs and nuzzled in between them, murmuring his approval. I lay there, pussy throbbing, pulling at my nipples, caressing my own breasts while my knees crushed his head as I tightened my grip, unable to believe a man could make me come in seconds.

He lapped at my juices as they oozed down his chin and then he was devouring me, driving me wild. I arched my back, peaking again, my nipples jutting forward as I pulled them harder, stretching and rolling them between my fingers as though offering them to him while my breathing became more laboured, more ragged.

He crushed a handful of strawberries, over my breasts and abdomen, smearing me with the pulp. As the sweetness drifted up to envelop me, my nostrils flared as his hand reached up and he slipped some fruit into my open mouth. I sucked on his fingers greedily, grinding my pussy against him but he pulled back and inserted something inside me; definitely not his cock, not hard or big enough to be that.

His mouth was back, licking my flaps, as he pushed whatever it was in and out of my pussy. I lifted my head to see but he was nibbling on my clit. As much as I didn't want him to stop I wanted to see what he was doing, so I pulled him away by the hair, his cheeky eyes staring at me over my mound and then with a quick munch at my pussy he was climbing up my body. He lowered his head to me with the distinct fragrance of banana all over him.

When he kissed me, the bitten-off piece of banana entered my mouth and we mashed it together, each of us biting into the fruit, sharing it in amorous longing for each other. His hand went into the pile of fruit and he smeared my body with cantaloupe, watermelon, and kiwi fruit.

I pulled him hard into me, pressing my body and the fruit all over him. We rolled around the blanket, laughing as we licked at the squashed fruit. Then he pinned me to the ground, pulling my arms up, holding them with one hand, forcing my chest to thrust upward as my stomach sucked in and my breasts beckoned him to them.

His eyes stared hard into mine.

'Open your legs,' he commanded.

I did, lying there quivering under his scrutiny while his cock pressed firmly into the side of my thigh. He ran his fingers down the inside of my arm, the side of my body and then over my mound.

'Hairless,' he breathed into my ear. 'There's nothing better.'

Letting go of my arms his hand roamed over my slit before his fingers probed my outer lips, pulling them open so his fat finger could snuggle under the hood to where my clit was hiding, waiting, anticipating his touch.

Electrified with passion, I reached for his cock, marvelling at the thickness of his shaft as my hand stroked and admired him. Precome was oozing from the slit. I lowered my head, flickered out my tongue and very gently licked his fabulous knob, my tongue lapping at the edges before my mouth hovered over the top of it. I moaned as my pussy pulsated madly, anticipating what was to come – namely me.

He threw me back down on the ground and I pulled him between my open thighs, inching my pussy closer to him, squirming until his knob was probing me. I held my breath, desperate for his magnificent cock to fill me up.

With one quick thrust he was fully inside me, going further than any man has ever been. He began pumping rhythmically and I swooned beneath him, my juices smearing his cock, wetting it so it slipped in and out deliciously. I pressed my open palm to his chest, pushing him away from me so I could peer down and watch the slippery monster glide in and out of me, rubbing against my bulging clit, swollen and throbbing, causing another orgasm to build up in me again.

I bucked back into him, wrapping my legs around his torso, kicking him with my heels, spurring him on. With a clenched fist I punched into him, overwhelmed with carnal lust, desperate for a good fucking.

He grabbed at my breasts, crushing them as his mouth came down to bite on my nipple. I screamed out in the still air as he sucked it into his mouth, fucking me harder. The horses neighed, momentarily startled. I punched into his back, crazy for more, wanting him to go on and on. I crushed my other breast but he knocked my hand away, eagerly sucking this nipple while pinching at the other one.

Pressure was building up inside me and I screamed even louder.

'Fuck me hard, you bastard. Harder!' I demanded.

He rolled on his back, lifting me with him. Straddling him like this, I ground down into him as he thrust upward. Punching my fists into his chest, I slammed down onto his groin, impaling myself, like a woman possessed.

'I can't get enough of you,' I screamed.

'You fucking horny little bitch.' He laughed, driving himself up into me.

Then he slapped me hard on the arse, the suddenness of it inflaming me more.

'Off,' he demanded.

'No.' I laughed, anticipating – no, hoping another slap at my disobedience would be coming.

'I said off,' he insisted.

'What?' I said, shocked and disappointed that he'd call a stop to the proceedings.

He grabbed my hand and dragged me to his horse. Naked, he swung up onto the saddle and I had a quick glimpse of his hairy balls as he threw his leg over.

'Here,' he said, holding out his hand to me.

'What?' I muttered.

'Your hand, come on. I promised you a ride you'll never forget.' He chuckled.

He hoisted me up and in a moment I was mounted upon him. It was high up there on the horse, and in this position, with his cock jutting upward; I was speared to the hilt upon him. Then suddenly he kicked his horse and it galloped off. He manoeuvred the reins while I hung on to him. Up and down I bounced, his cock hitting inside me so hard I was sure my lungs would be bruised.

'This is madness,' I screamed.

He laughed, deep in his throat, and I fleetingly wondered if we really were alone up here. Imagine someone coming across us like this? Watching us as we galloped along. Just thinking about it was turning me on even more.

I wrapped my legs around his back, smothering his face in between my breasts as I held on to his head. He lifted me by the hips and as the horse galloped along he held me aloft so with each galloping step his cock was forced up harder into me. He bit down on a nipple and I screamed out, enjoying being naked and alone out here.

I was delirious, being fucked like never before. There's nothing in this world that can compare to it. It made for the most amazing sex. I was screaming as I came all over his cock and he roared with laughter as my juices oozed into his groin and over the saddle. Then he gripped me tightly, his fingers digging into my cheeks, as he came in torrents, filling me up as the horse slowly cantered back to the blanket and then stopped.

We slid off the saddle and fell onto the blanket and into each other's arms. The earthy smells that surrounded us held us deep in their fragrance as we lay there, cocooned in this wonderful place while our breathing returned to normal. My breath caught in my throat, pleased when his hand began to roam over me and with renewed strength we were at it again.

Then I was up on all fours with him behind me, ramming into me, his fingers gripping my hips as he slammed back in. I pushed back eagerly, wanting every inch of his massive cock inside me as my head flung itself around like a rag-doll.

He pulled out of me and I whipped myself around to take his wet and slippery cock into my hungry mouth. I licked and sucked, saliva running down my chin, until I thought my mouth would split, the girth of his cock was so huge. Then I was begging, begging him to take me back on the horse and fuck me as we rode naked through the countryside.

'Back on all fours,' he demanded. 'I want to fuck your arse.'

'Not a chance in hell,' I said, 'with a monster like that. You'll split me in two.'

'On all fours,' he said again.

'You're joking.' I half laughed.

'Never been more serious.'

'It'll never fit,' I complained.

'It will.'

Seeing how serious he was I had to ask, 'You won't hurt me, will you?'

'No.'

Trusting him, I did as he asked. With my arse in the air he knelt down and gently licked at the cheeks. He did this for quite some time until I began to relax. Then his tongue slid down the crack of my arse, up and down, even slipping into my cunt a few time. It was heavenly.

I felt his fingers pull my cheeks slowly apart and still his tongue was rimming me, slathering me with saliva before a finger slipped in.

'Nice?' he asked.

'Yes,' I whispered.

He pushed in deeper, finger-fucking me.

'Oh God, yes,' I moaned. I'd had this done before and quite enjoyed it but no one had ever had their cock up there.

'You like it, don't you?' he chuckled.

'Oh yeah, especially when you do it like that,' I said.

One of his other fingers was grazing my snatch, slipping in between the folds so much so that I couldn't concentrate on what he was doing which was obviously what he'd intended.

The next thing I knew his thumbs were digging into my cheeks and his knob was probing my puckered hole. I clenched but he slapped my cheek hard.

'Relax,' he ordered.

I did but cheekily clenched again, pleased when I received another smack and then another. I pushed back a little and felt the knob slip in. I couldn't believe it would fit. I peered over my shoulder at him.

'I told you I wouldn't hurt you.' He smiled, as his hands gripped my hips and he slowly began to push his way in.

I must admit I tensed again, unable to believe it wouldn't hurt. But true to his word it didn't and I found myself pushing back harder, enjoying the sensation of my first time at arse fucking. Before long he was slamming into me and I can't explain it exactly, can't explain what it did to me but it made me have the most powerful of orgasms, so much so that my knees buckled and I almost collapsed on my arms from the sheer magnitude of it.

When he'd had his fill he gently pulled himself from me and cradled me in his arms.

'That was the best fuck I've ever had,' he said.

'Me too,' I whispered.

'You want to go back?'

'Not yet. How about another go on the horse? I loved that,' I begged.

'Your wish is my command.'

And, like Prince Charming, he mounted the horse and then had me mount him, taking us down to the still secluded beach. With no one about we fucked as the horse galloped through the ocean, cold sprays of water causing me to squeal in delight.

Finally, three hours later, totally satisfied, we dressed and make our way home with no one the wiser.

I've promised to go back again, soon, very soon, and next time I do I'll be bringing back my movie camera.

With a cock like Jeff's I'm sure I could spend hours keeping myself amused – but, more importantly, I want to be able to show all my friends back home exactly how well the studs are hung in New Zealand, and by that I don't mean the horses.

Productivity
by K D Grace

'You want me to do what?' Alan's voice cracked in a sudden bout of nerves that would have been completely unacceptable at the negotiating table.

'You heard me.' Victoria spoke like she had just asked him to hand her the stapler. 'I'd give you a little privacy and let you do it in the loo, but you'd tell me you'd done it when you actually hadn't, and then you'd go into this meeting with the muscles in your shoulders still like rocks and the acid in your stomach still on the rise.' She walked to the door like she owned the place and locked it. 'It's my job to prevent that, so come on,' she nodded to the fly of his trousers. 'Trust me, you'll feel so much better afterward, and you'll be amazed at how much better the meeting will go.'

He folded his hands protectively in his lap. 'I can't just yank one off right here in front of you.'

'Course you can. I've got a copy of *Hustler* in my briefcase if that'll help.'

He cursed under his breath and scooted as far back in his chair as he could get.

She rolled her eyes. 'Look, you hired me to improve your productivity, to make you a better boss, and frankly, you've got no outlet.'

'I'm going to the gym three times a week, just like you ordered. That's an outlet, isn't it?'

She tisk-tisked him. 'Alan, you told me yourself you haven't had a good shag in four years.'

'Three and a half,' he corrected.

She waved a dismissive hand. 'The point is, humans are sexual animals, we have sexual needs, and whether you like it or not, the fact that yours aren't getting met interferes with your productivity.'

'You don't know that.'

She gave him a hard stare over the top of her Sarah Palin glasses. 'Look, when you hired me, a part of the deal was that you do as I say. I told you I'm too busy to waste my time with someone who isn't serious about taking my advice.'

'I know, but ...'

'You knew my methods were unorthodox. You also know that I'm the best. I get the job done when no one else can.'

'Yes, but –'

'Then do it.' She looked down at her watch. 'You've got plenty of time. I planned it that way so you could relax and enjoy it.' She raised a hand to squelch his protest. 'Don't tell me you need to go over your presentation. That's rubbish. We both know you don't. You probably have it memorised. I promise you, this will be much more beneficial than reviewing your notes.' She nodded again to his fly.

When he still sat frozen in his seat, she heaved a busty sigh, grabbed a chair and pulled it in front of his. 'If it'll help, I'll do it with you. Will that be better?' She was already pulling her pencil skirt up over her hips to reveal red lace suspenders and knickers that were barely there. All at once it felt like the air had gone out of the office, and the sudden bulge in his trousers threatened to blow a seam.

'There. You see?' She nodded to his expanding package. 'If it takes no more than a look at my knickers to make you hard, then I'd say I've proven my point.' She unbuttoned her blouse to reveal a matching bra. 'Hope you don't mind, but when I masturbate, I like to play with my breasts.'

Play with her breasts! Bloody hell! For a terrifying moment, he thought he would lose control and come right there in his trousers.

'Breathe,' she commanded, as she reached behind her to undo her bra. 'There's no rush. Take your time. Enjoy it.' She released full breasts topped with gumdrop nipples, and her gaze dipped again to his crotch. 'It you don't relieve the pressure down there, you'll rip the zipper out.'

This time, he obeyed, struggling first with his belt, which threatened to defeat him now that all the blood had left his brain and rushed to his cock.

'Relax,' her voice was suddenly thicker, lazier, like she'd just gotten out of bed. 'There's nothing to be nervous about. Your task is to enjoy yourself.' She cupped her breasts and began to knead, stroking the length of her nipples between thumbs and forefingers. 'You're the boss, remember? All good bosses have their secret weapons, and sex is the very best one, I promise you.'

'But with myself?' He sucked oxygen between his teeth as his cock sprang free, pointing accusingly toward Victoria's haughty nipples.

'Sex is sex. It doesn't matter if it's a solo job, as long as it gets results.' Her eyes locked on his erection. 'Now stroke it, the way you like most. You do have a favourite method, don't you, a way that makes you come best? Most people do, at least the ones who are honest.'

'You make all your clients masturbate?' he grunted.

'If they're not coming regularly, yes. You'd be surprised what a common problem that is.'

Even then he would have hesitated, but she wriggled down in the chair to get comfortable. Then she raised the half-dome cheeks of her luscious bottom just enough to pull the crotch of her panties out of the way and give him a view of the smoothly shaven split that began against the pale pillow of her mound and opened, as her legs splayed, to reveal dark, moist folds protecting the swell of her pout between. Then, the no-nonsense fingers that handled a BlackBerry like a surgeon's scalpel slipped in between those distended folds and began to thrust and scissor in long, lazy strokes, pausing periodically to tweak her clit against the press of her thumb.

By that time his cock felt like a zeppelin between his legs, and the weight in his balls was unbearable. He couldn't stand it any longer. He began yanking and tugging at himself like there was no tomorrow, grinding and bouncing against the chair until he feared he'd split the leather. All the while, his gaze never left her pussy, where her thrusting fingers perfectly matched his rhythm.

It was all over in a few breathless seconds. He arched in the chair as though his back would break and shot a jet-powered stream of jizz arcing across the floor straight onto her smart, black stilettos.

But before he managed more than a flash of embarrassment, she stiffened against the probing of her fingers and uttered a little mewling cry that quivered up her throat and erupted into a sharp gasp.

Then she was kneeling in front of him with the box of tissues helping him clean up and tucking him in, all the while speaking a throaty string of encouragements. 'That was good, Alan. Well done. Just what you needed. You'll knock 'em dead.'

And he did! The impossible client was putty in his hand, and the deal went through with more ease than he could have ever hoped for.

'You see. You negotiated from a position of power,' she said afterward during their debriefing. 'And having a good come always puts one in the position of power. You're the alpha wolf, Alan. You get to shoot your wad while others have to hold it.' She paced back and forth in front of his desk, the navy pencil skirt now hiding the red suspenders and knickers. They might be well hidden, but he knew they were there, and that made it hard to concentrate on what she was saying.

'Never underestimate the power of being the one who gets to come,' she was saying.

'But it was just a wank.' He shifted in his chair, feeling as though he could use another one.

She turned to face him. 'Was it?'

He blushed. 'I came on your shoes.'

She leant forward over his desk, both hands flat against the blotter, leant so far forward that they were practically nose to nose. It took only the slightest dip of his eyes to glimpse red lace cupping her breasts, and suddenly he was uncomfortably stiff again. Her lipsticked full mouth curled into a knowing smile. 'Doesn't matter. You made me come, didn't you?'

'Did you masturbate after you got home last night?' It was the first question she asked him the next morning when they were settled into his office for a look at the day's agenda.

'God, Victoria, couldn't you wait until I've at least had my tea?'

'Well? Did you?'

He fiddled with his laptop, hoping she wouldn't notice the rising blush. 'I did,' came the curt reply. Twice, in fact, but he didn't tell her that. He felt a surge in his trousers as he recalled thinking about her while he yanked and stroked and cupped himself to two more big ones before he fell asleep, and then the rest of the night he fucked her in the dream world. God, he hoped she didn't ask any more questions.

'Good, excellent. Good work, Alan. I think we're making some real progress here. I'm very pleased with your success.'

He didn't know how the woman did it, but somehow she made him feel really proud to be such a good wanker.

There was no more mention of masturbation for the rest of the week. She went with him to the warehouse and took lots of notes. She checked the filing systems and took even more notes. She questioned him about his preparations for a big meeting early next week. And every night, after he got home, he masturbated, imagining her mouth on his cock, imagining coming with his cock pressed between the swell of her tits, imagining her bent over his desk, skirt hiked, knickers pushed aside to reveal her pussy, all swollen and pouting and gagging for him.

When the day of the big meeting came, they sat facing each other in his office, her with her legs crossed demurely to support the notepad she'd been writing on. She scribbled something across the page then smiled up at him. 'I'll trust you to go off to the loo for a little privacy this time, if you'd like.'

But he was already undoing his belt. 'Not necessary. When a man's come on a woman's shoes, there's a certain bond that develops between them, don't you think?'

She chuckled softly. 'Good point.' Almost as though it had a mind of its own, her hand moved over her jacket to brush against her breasts. Nearly unnoticeable beneath the power suit, her hips shifted against the seat and she sat forward slightly as though she were anticipating his presentation. As he released his rapidly expanding cock and squirmed to free his balls into the cup of one hand, her eyes never left his crotch. She sat quietly with her legs still crossed. One hand had moved inside her jacket and he imagined she was stroking an erect nipple through the silk blouse.

'That's good, Alan. Well done,' she whispered as she watched him thrust and rock against his hand. 'You're magnificent when you're hard, when you're touching yourself, stroking your balls. Everyone needs to come, Alan. They're all waiting to shoot their wad. But only the alpha wolves get to come. Remember that. Only the alpha wolves.'

Her jacket had fallen open to reveal her enthusiastic kneading of her breasts, the hard pinching of her nipples, and the obvious fact that she wasn't wearing a bra. She fumbled with the buttons on her blouse and ran a hand inside. A sigh trembled over her lips as her hand cupped and kneaded bare flesh.

And he was suddenly an exhibitionist in a way he could have never imagined himself – him always so conservative, always so buttoned down. He pumped hard against his hand, imagining her pussy tightening around him, imagining the slick grip of her. He shoved his trousers down over his hips until his bare arse rubbed and slid against leather.

'You're full, aren't you, Alan?' Her voice was becoming more breathless. 'It arouses you what you're about to do in that conference room, doesn't it? Your balls ache with the weight of it, the anticipation of it. But you can't go in there like this. You can't think with your cock. So now's the time to take care of it, then you'll go in relaxed and ready. You're almost there, I can tell. Come for me, Alan. Empty your balls for me, and it'll be so good, I promise.'

And just when he was about to burst, she moved next to him and caught his wad in a soft cotton handkerchief, gently wiping and stroking him clean while he struggled to catch his breath.

'There, now. That's so much better, isn't it? You came so good. And now,' she carefully folded the handkerchief and stuck it in the pocket of her jacket, giving him just a glimpse of bare breast as she did so, 'you're all set.'

The meeting had been a complete success followed by dinner and drinks to celebrate. It was only after everyone had been safely tucked in taxis and sent home mildly but happily drunk that Alan realised he'd left his briefcase at the office. As he exited the lift, he was still thinking about the uncanny successes of the past week and wondering if sex – even solo sex – really had anything to do with it. The rustling of cloth and a moan startled him and he stopped in his tracks across from the darkened conference room. There was another rustle and a soft buzz. Cautiously, he pushed the door open and peeked inside. He was greeted by the sound of Victoria's voice.

'Either come in or stay out, but shut the door.'

As he pulled the door to behind him, the buzzing became more prominent in the darkness.

'Lock it, would you? Sorry, I forgot to. I wasn't expecting company at this hour.' Her voice was breathless, strained, and as his eyes adjusted to the dark, he understood why.

She sat on the end of the conference table with her legs splayed, stilettoed feet resting on the arms of the chair at the head of the table.

Her shirt was open and her breasts forced upward over the top of a pale lace bra, nipples at attention from the hard press. Her skirt was up over her hips and the crotch of her panties was shoved unceremoniously aside to make room for a hefty penis-shaped vibrator which was buried to the hilt and buzzing enthusiastically in her grasping pussy. With her free hand, she tweaked and rubbed at her clit, all the while rocking and shifting precariously on the edge of the table.

She must have noticed the shocked look on his face. She forced a breathy laugh. 'You're not the only alpha wolf,' she grunted. 'Nor are you the only one who doesn't have time for a shag.'

'I didn't know.' He felt stupid the minute he'd said it, but he couldn't think of anything else to say. In fact, he found it difficult to think of anything but the way her pussy sucked and gripped the penis-shaped vibrator, which he was certain, was not nearly as hard as his own cock had suddenly become.

'Is this your chair, the chair where you make the big decisions?' She spoke between thrusts, nodding to the chair between her legs.

'Yes,' he rasped.

She ground her arse hard against the table. 'You can sit down, if you want.'

'Thank you. I'd like that.'

Without missing a thrust, she lifted one leg to give him room, and he settled into the chair, taking in the mouth-watering scent of hot pussy and a view that he had fantasised about all week as she brought her foot back down to rest on his shoulder.

'You should probably undo your trousers. I imagine they're struggling for containment.'

He didn't have to be told twice. Once his cock was free, he began to stroke, matching her rhythm as she thrust herself onto the dildo. He had drank just enough wine and the situation was just surreal enough to make him bold. 'Lose the vibrator,' he commanded. 'I want to look at you.'

The buzzing stopped. 'You'll have to do more than look if you want me to take it out.'

'Then I'll take it out.' He slapped her hand away and slowly eased the vibrator free, feeling her hungry grip tighten, relax and tighten again until, in one last gripping pull, she released the length of it with a shudder. He tossed it onto the floor, then opened her heavy lips with the pads of his thumbs and felt her hips shift forward, pressing in until she was millimetres from his face. The temptation was more than he could resist. He ran his tongue from just above the dark clench of her anus, feeling her squirm, feeling her soft moans and grunts vibrate all the way down through her perineum as he licked and nipped his way up her, flicking his tongue as deep into her gash as he could manage, then moving upward to suckle and nip her clit. She grabbed at his hair, pulling him closer, bucking against him, drenching his face in the sweet flavour of her, all the while making lovely inarticulate sounds at the back of her throat.

'Fuck me,' she gasped, as though she had just surfaced from a long time under water. 'I need you to fuck me now.'

He rose from the chair, holding her open for a better look at the ravenous grasping of her. He caressed her clit, making her quiver before he lifted her bottom off the table toward his pointing cock. 'Will this help productivity?'

'Yours and mine,' she said.

He shoved his hands under the clenching muscles of her arse and lifted her until the angle was just right. Then he inched into her slowly, feeling her yield and grip and yield again like she had done on the dildo. When she was completely impaled, she wrapped her legs around him and pulled him to her.

'You taste like me,' she sighed against his mouth.

'Then I taste good,' he replied, lowering his mouth to her jutting nipples, sucking hard and biting just enough to make her gasp. And when she gasped, she bore down, and her cunt gripped him like a closed fist.

He shoved and pushed his way onto the table, on top of her, feeling her lacquered nails claw at his shoulders before she scrabbled backward to grab the outer edges of the table for leverage against his pounding.

'If we break the table,' she gasped, as he humped and ground into the vice of her, 'you'll have some explaining to do tomorrow.'

'I'm the boss,' he replied, giving her an extra hard hunch. 'I don't have to explain anything.'

Her throaty laugh ended in a growl, and suddenly she was clawing and wrestling and kneeing until he yielded and she forced her way on top. She sat straddling him in the middle of the big table, leaning forward, pinning his arms over his head. Her impossibly tight nipples bounced temptingly at mouth level as she began to gyrate against him. Her bottom shifted and shoved, massaging his balls. With each rocking, each gyration they felt fuller and heavier, until they could barely contain their load.

Almost as though she knew just that, she tightened her already impossible grip and bore down until he cried out and began to thrust back in a frenzy, like the friction had lit fire that had to be quenched. It wasn't just her hungry snatch sucking at his cock. It was everything – the smell of pussy and sweat and expensive perfume. The salty sweet after-taste of her still on his tongue, the little grunts and cries she made that became growls with her expanding passion. The table trembled and creaked beneath them as they bucked and grunted ever harder.

'This is it,' she hissed between her teeth. 'The ideal. Two alpha wolves coming together. It's what you need. What we both need.' The howl that escaped her throat wasn't unlike that of a wolf as her whole body spasmed and shook with her orgasm.

The vibration of her, the trembling and convulsing of her was more than he could take. He came hard. He came like he'd never stop, with her gripping him like she'd never let go.

The next morning, she was waiting for him in his office as usual. She wore a charcoal power suit, with matching stilettos. Her hair was scraped back in a no-nonsense ponytail. The briefcase of cordovan leather sat open on her lap. The alpha wolf was well-disguised, he thought. Then he reminded himself that he looked at least as dapper and well-disguised as she did. He offered her his best professional smile. 'Good morning, Victoria.'

'Good morning, Alan.'

He nodded to the briefcase. 'What's on the productivity agenda for today?'

She looked up at him over the top of her glasses. 'It's the files, Alan. I've been thinking about the files ever since you showed me your system.' She leant forward and he caught a hint of lace pressed against the inside of her silk blouse. 'This is not a job you need to be doing. Delegate it. You're the boss. You're time is too valuable to spend being a glorified file clerk.'

'All right. I can do that.' As he shifted in the chair, the tight bulge in his pocket reminded him of one of her earlier lectures about not taking himself quite so seriously, and he smiled.

'What?'

He reached into his pocket and pulled out the penis-shaped vibrator. 'You forgot this in the conference room last night. Understandable under the circumstances.'

She offered him a crooked smile. A hint of a blush crawled up her throat as she took the vibrator from him. 'Wouldn't want to forget that, would I? After all, one never knows when it might be advantageous to come.'

He held her gaze as she slipped the vibrating cock into her briefcase. 'One never knows, does one?' He felt the familiar tightening in his trousers. Perhaps even the delegation of the filing was a task that might go better after a good come.

Just Like Your Father
by Sommer Marsden

'And this is Carlene. She worked with your father for five years. She'll be able to give you just about anything you need.' Zoey smiled at Eli. Eli felt nothing but panic.

He smiled, swallowed it down and shook hands with the woman he guessed to be about five years his senior. 'I hope that means you make magic happen.'

Carlene laughed, long, cool fingers playing over his as she withdrew her hand. 'I try. I don't think I make magic, but I do make things happen.'

'I can attest to that!' Zoey said. 'But now I'll leave you two to get to know each other. I have a presentation to give down on the third floor. Nervous is not a big enough word to cover it.'

'You'll do great, Zoey, just remember the most important thing.'

'Drink?'

'Breathe!' Carlene touched Zoey's arm and off she went, into the wild workplace.

'I hope that goes for me too,' Eli admitted.

'You'll do great too, Eli. What seems foreign today will be second nature in a month.'

'From your lips ...' Eli said with a nervous laugh.

'When you laugh you sound just like your father. Now let's start easy. Phone system?'

'Hey, might as well.'

When he sat in the chair he felt like an impostor. A little boy sitting in his father's place, playing make-believe. When Carlene leant across his back and started to push buttons, he felt giddy. With the smell of her perfume – sandalwood and peaches – his body hummed to life. She was gorgeous – lush and ripe with dark brown hair that glowed with good health and a sturdy brushing. He imagined she could give a really good ...

'–this one puts you right back to me after,' she declared and he looked up into her smiling face, her bright blue eyes twinkling with good humour.

Eli felt his eyes do a fast detour down her slender neck to the swell of her cleavage – tasteful, but present – the pinch of her waist, the flare of her hips. The decadent way her body curved that made his tongue feel about two sizes too big.

'Sorry?'

'I said if you want to put someone on hold and then talk to me you press this one,' she pushed a button gently using his finger instead of her own. Her hand wrapped around his and Eli felt his cock tent his charcoal grey pants.

Great. Offend the woman who runs the show by getting an erection because she touched your hand. Because you are ... oh ... 14, Eli!

He gritted his teeth and tried to focus. He caught Carlene watching him and nodded as if it made all the sense in the world. 'I push this and then ...'

Carlene moved his hand to another button, this one green. 'This one,' she said.

'Right.' He pretended to push the button, which made him think of her clit, which made him think of burrowing his head beneath that proper skirt to see if she had on full stockings or thigh highs. Or was she old school and sporting garters and panties and ... This wasn't helping.

'When you get flustered, you look just like your father,' she said right up to his ear and Eli felt a rush of goosebumps across his neck and shoulders.

'You worked a lot with my dad?'

Carlene nodded, and moved to the other side of his desk. There. That was good. He was safe now. She was *alllllllll* the way over there.

'We worked closely. Especially on a few big projects. Penski, Stewart, Toye ...' she rattled off names that meant nothing to Eli. Aerospace might as well be gene splicing for all he knew about it.

'Good, good. I'll need help.'

Carlene smiled and said, 'I'll give you anything you need that you think will help, Eli.'

Blowjob? ... no, no, no! You perv. Stop!

Eli cleared his throat and tugged his collar. 'Erm, thanks, Carlene. You're a gem.'

'No problem. Now I'll just go and get–' Her sleeve, a festive bell-shaped sleeve that made Eli think of fancy women dancing in big ballrooms, caught his pencil cup and tumbled the contents to the ground. 'Oh!'

'Let me help,' Eli said. He felt so much better now that she'd done something imperfect. It helped him breathe and be calm. She was not infallible and he didn't have to live up to his father's shadow. He just had to be himself. He was running the sales and overseeing for Richardson Aerospace, not building the parts.

Together they crawled around on the floor, picking up pencils. Eli's eyes would stray to the gorgeous swell of Carlene's ass and then he'd bite his tongue to focus. He saw a flash of thigh, a flex of calf, and yes – sweet merciful Lord – a garter and the lacy top of a stocking.

Awesome, now I can drive nails with my dick ...

'There. I think that's all of them,' she said, brushing the fluffs of dark hair from her face. 'I'm sorry. I'm really clumsy sometimes.'

'Me too,' he admitted.

Carlene touched his hand and said 'Just like your father ...' and shook her head with a smile. 'He spilt more coffee than any man I knew. And dropped pencils. Papers. Everything!'

So he could watch your fine ass when you bent over to pick them up. He's no fool, the old man ...

'It must be an inherited trait.' He swallowed hard and averted his eyes. This woman was going to be the gateway to his success. Not a good thing to take pleasure where you should be doing business.

'I'll leave you to look over paperwork. I'll be right out here. I have some reports to type up and some files that need attention. A recent temp put financials for one vendor in another's file and so on. It's a mess.'

'Right. Good stuff. Carry on. I don't mean to hold you up.'

She blinked, looking sorry for him and then bent to retrieve one more stray pencil. Eli got a dizzying glimpse of a valley of creamy cleavage and he thought he might actually expire in his father's big, poufy swivel chair. He shut his eyes to stop his heart-rate from climbing.

'You're no bother and no hold up. Such a worrywart,' she said. 'And handsome. Just like your father.'

Hmm. What else has this little minx done with my father?

But he shook his head and shooed her. 'Go on, be productive. One of us should be.'

She went with a healthy swing of her luscious ass and Eli briefly considered locking the door and beating off, but then thought better of it. Probably not a good idea your first day "in charge" to get caught spanking the monkey, so to speak.

He sat and pored over thick important documents and spreadsheets that glowed gruesomely on his screen, mocking him for not understanding. 'Might as well be written in Greek,' he growled, feeling frustrated and impotent and like he wanted to just hit someone, or something.

'You'll get it,' she said from the doorway, looking like a vision. 'Brought you some coffee.'

Her nylons whispered secretively as she crossed the room and Eli had a brief flash of peeling them off of her long, long legs. Carlene made him a cup of coffee without asking his preference and when Eli tasted it, it was the best fucking cup of coffee he'd ever had. Probably because she'd made it, but that was neither here nor there. 'Thank you.'

'You just need to relax,' she said. 'May I?' she nodded toward the empty visitor chair.

'Oh, please!'

Carlene wrestled it close so that her chair pressed his and Eli was wildly aware of the warm scent of her and her outrageous body that seemed to push against the restrain of her proper clothes. 'You just need to highlight the intended amount and that shows you how much has been ordered and for what quarter ...'

He lost her voice then because his pulse had jacked up so high all he could hear was his loud heart and the dry click in his throat when he swallowed. She caught his gaze and said, 'You really do need to calm down.' She sounded like she was at the far end of a long tunnel.

'I don't know how,' Eli said, giving himself fully to the panic.

'Hmm. Let's see.' She dropped to her knees right

there, pushing him back on his wheeled chair. Eli was thankful for that chair because, without it, he surely would have fallen on his ass and he had finally – it seemed – started to hallucinate. 'What can we do about that?' Carlene asked and undid his zipper.

'The door?' he said numbly.

'Is locked,' she answered.

And then his cock was in her hand and her lips followed swiftly. Glossy pink lips that sucked the head of his cock deep and a warm, wet tongue that swirled in dizzying loops around his shaft. She sucked him deep and her fingers played along the base of him with cool efficiency. She handled his balls gently but sucked madly and within moments a load of stress rushed out of him and he was touching her soft, soft hair.

'Stand up.' Eli's voice finally sounded commanding and her big blue eyes found his. She smiled, his cock still in her mouth, and he thought he'd come if she didn't stop right then. 'Now.'

She stood in front of him and Eli ran his hands along the valleys and peaks of her body. He pinched a nipple through her crisp white blouse, feeling the lace of her bra underneath. But her nipple rose up and she made a soft sound that made him feel a bit crazed.

Eli hiked up her skirt and pushed his face to the cream-coloured knickers underneath. He felt the warmth of her sex on his cheek and she pushed her fingers into his hair. Oddly, he found that he had the urge to stay right here until his body and mind calmed. Instead, he pressed his lips to the gusset of her panties and breathed out, while worming a finger under the elastic and testing her cunt.

God, she was wet. God, how he wanted her. This was *so* much better than masturbation in a locked office.

He made a slow ritual of undoing her garters, peeling

77

her panties down, leaving her garter belt in place so that the elastics swung festively. As he rolled down her stockings, she said, 'See, you can do a meticulous job when you calm down.'

'Good point.' Her pussy lips were slick and soft and he sucked one and then the other before locating the swollen nub of her clit with the tip of his tongue. Eli drove two fingers deep and curled the tips against the wet suede flesh deep inside her.

'Oh,' she said as if in mid conversation.

'Yes, oh.' He sucked and licked until her body grew taut and her fingers bit into his scalp and, when she came, he felt the ripple work through her cunt and her body shivered with it. 'Now, about bending over that desk.'

'Yes, sir,' she said, her laughter sweet to his ears.

Eli parted her legs, studying the swell of her ass, the puckered star of her anus, the wet split of her pussy and he drove himself deep into her inch by inch, his fingertip playing her back hole until she squirmed under him like a cat in heat. It was the hottest thing he'd ever seen. 'You're so wet.'

'I am.'

'And tight.'

'Good.'

'And hot.'

'Yes,' she said.

'I'm going to come,' he admitted.

She worked a hand under her and Eli watched her tendons flex as she rubbed her clit in time with his thrusts. He gripped her flared hips tightly, relishing the jiggle of her bottom as he fucked her. When her pussy clamped up around him again, he let himself go. Dropping backwards into his orgasm like a man dropping into a pool.

The orgasm ripped through him and when it had

passed, he dropped to his knees, feeling a bit weak. He kissed the back of each of her pale thighs and then watched her calmly put herself back together.

She dropped into his lap and kissed him softly. 'Feel better?'

Eli nodded. 'I do. And let me guess. I did that just like my father.'

Her face clouded. 'Oh, I wouldn't know. I never did *that* with your father.'

'So just me?' So sue him, he felt a rush of glee at the information.

'Yes. Just you. I have to admit, I found you attractive from the get-go.'

Something swelled in his chest and he nodded, ready to tackle his difficult first day. 'Great. I'm thrilled.' He gave her a kiss and said, 'Now about ordering lunch?'

'I'll get right on it.'

'And then I'll need your help with this database. So I can decipher it.'

'No problem,' she said, all business again.

'Oh, and Carlene?'

'Sir?'

'When you come back with the food, lock the door. I have a feeling this database is going to stress me out a lot.'

She smiled and it went straight to his dick. 'We can't have that now, can we?'

'No. No, ma'am, we can't,' Eli said and sat back in his poufy swivel chair. It was good to be the boss.

You Get What You Pay For
by J Smith

My husband Mark had always been adventurous in bed, and I hadn't been surprised by the fact he liked role play, I mean we all do but when he told me he had always fantasised about paying for sex with a slutty-looking pro I was a bit shocked. It wasn't until I played along with it that I discovered that I fitted right into the role.

So here I was standing on the street corner, waiting. I was dressed in a T-shirt, too tight and no bra, and my leather mini skirt with no knickers, well it saved time. My leather boots finished the image and were the only things keeping me warm.

A few cars had slowed as they passed me, you knew what the men were wondering, how much and what I'd do, but I had a select client tonight and wasn't open to the public. Even so, to know that they were thinking of me in a dirty little scenario up some back alley got my nipples stiffer than the evening breeze.

I took another drag on my cigarette as I looked up the road. I saw the car coming, Mark's red BMW. I moved to the kerb, and pushed my chest out, my tits weren't the biggest but they had the perfect shape, round with their own uplift, like a couple of cherry-topped buns.

The car pulled up and the window came down.

'You looking for business?' Mark said. He was attractive with his dark hair and designer stubble, straight from an office with his tie and jacket still on.

'If you have the money,' I replied and watched him look me up and down, his eyes feeling their way across my breasts and down my legs. It felt exciting, getting picked up in the street, sex for money. It was the fact that it was so sordid, taboo. I didn't know what he was going to want me to do, but if he could afford it I was up for it. I always was.

He looked in his rear view mirror to see if anyone had spotted him and then he opened the passenger door and told me to get in. He tried to look up my skirt as I sat down and by the way his eyes widened I think he saw the parting of the waves. I could tell how desperate he was by the large bulge in his trousers, he must have been thinking about me all the way here. I flicked my cigarette out the window and we drove off.

He said nothing and we turned from the main road and into the deserted car park of a trading estate. He stopped the engine and turned to me.

'So what's it to be?' I asked suggestively and breathed deep to push my bust out.

'I don't know.' His mind was on my tight T-shirt and what it was struggling to hold in.

'Well it's the usual on offer. Hand job, blowjob, full sex or tricks if you feel really naughty.' I slowly rubbed the head of the gear stick and he looked like a boy in a sweet shop, spoilt for choice. The telltale stain of pre-come darkening his trousers also told me he was desperate.

He looked at my painted lips, 'Blowjob. Suck me off.' He eagerly started to undo his flies.

'Money first,' I told him. 'Twenty-five pounds.' Not that I didn't want to see his manhood but rules are rules. He fumbled for his wallet and handed over the notes which I scrunched up into a pocket.

He finished undoing his flies and thrust his hips up towards me.

'I bet you're quite big,' I put my hand inside and started to draw him out. 'Oh yes. You're going to be quite a mouthful.'

I ran my hand up and down his shaft, letting it throb between my fingers.

'Suck it. Suck it hard.'

Well what else could I do? He'd paid for it. I licked my lips, opened my mouth and lowered it over his exposed knob. He groaned as I sank around him, and he thrust himself deeper into the moist warmth of my mouth. He tasted so good and I felt so dirty sucking him in the front seat of his car. I wondered how many security cameras were zoomed in on me right now, how many eyes were watching. I could feel my pussy swell with juice.

He groaned some more and I had to control his cock with my hand as it gagged at the back of my throat. His length flashed in and out of me, my tongue flicking at it as I sucked it back in and he watched every second. His fingers felt for my stiff nips and began to squeeze them, stretch them out. He spasmed in my mouth, I knew he wouldn't last much longer. I slowly opened my legs and let him see my scarlet slit, glistening with my love dew. As soon as he saw it, he came. His cock twitched in my mouth and he bit on his lip to stifle his cry. A stream of his warm come splashed against the back of my throat and I greedily swallowed it down, and then another, I sucked hard as if I was trying to get the last drop of juice from an orange and I didn't stop until he'd been drained. Then I lifted my head from him and licked my lips.

He sat back and let his contented smile tell me how

good I'd been.

'How was that?' I asked.

'You were great, as usual.'

'I know,' I said. 'Now let's go home, I need a good fuck in my own bed. Oh and that's five pounds for swallowing,' I said jokingly.

Once home Mark was ready for action again, we didn't make it to the bed. As soon as we got in he hitched my skirt up and took me against the hall wall, thrusting his length inside me with my legs tightly wrapped around his waist. It was fast but fantastic. For the time being he seemed satisfied and the orgasm that had shot through my body had left me more than happy.

We sat down, had a drink and started chatting about the day. I told him about the other men who had tried to pick me up on the street, about how some of them were good looking, I teased him by saying that if he hadn't turned up I might have gone with them. What he said took me by surprise.

'That's not such a bad idea.'

'What?' I wasn't sure I'd heard him.

'Well, if you fancy them.'

'You want me to pick some stranger up off the street and let them fuck me … for money.'

He smiled wickedly. 'Yeah. That's what I want.'

'And you'll get off on this how?'

'I'll be watching.'

I couldn't believe he was asking me to do it. Dressing up for him was one thing but for real … with Mark watching, I mean it was just perverse, it was so grubby, it was so … turning me on.

'Won't this other man think it a bit weird you're watching?'

'No, I'll be hiding or something.'

'I'm not sure,' but I could feel my pulse start to race.

'You want to, don't you?' he said. 'The way you were talking about those men I could see it written all over your face. I bet you wanted them to take you from behind over the bonnet. Any cock will do as long as it's hard.'

'That's not the point … fantasy is one thing but … you actually want to watch me with another man?'

'No. I want to see you get paid for sex.'

'And he can do whatever I let him, no matter what?'

'If he pays for extras the dirtier the better.'

I couldn't believe I was actually contemplating it and I couldn't believe the size Mark's cock had got since talking about it. He was almost coming again just thinking about it.

'Just do it once, for me,' he pleaded. 'Any trouble and I can stop it.'

'I don't know,' I told him. 'I'd have to think about it,' and in explicit detail.

Within two days we had a plan. I would pick someone up from one of the bars around the corner. That way it would be me in charge of who I had, then I would bring them back to the main bedroom in the flat. Mark was going to set up his web cam and watch it all from the spare room and probably wank himself stupid. I made a note to buy an extra box of tissues.

We would do it this coming Friday, loads of businessmen fed up and wanting to unwind before going home. Shouldn't be too difficult.

Friday came. Mark had even had some business cards made up for me. He'd invented the name "Chloe" for me and had it printed next to the silhouette of a naked woman, double Es at least, underneath this was the slogan "Personal Pleasures". That should do the trick.

Next problem was what to wear. I seemed to be going more for escort than street girl but either way I had to look hot and available, they had to know what they were getting. I chose my red stilettos, short red dress, up to my arse and down to my navel, hold ups with a seam and a black thong with red trim. I didn't let Mark know what I was wearing, let it be a surprise for him.

Friday evening came. Mark set up the camera and waited in the room. I got ready and made my way to the bar. My heart was beating like a sparrow's as I opened the door. It was full of men and all of them looked at me, undressing me with their eyes. I played the part and kept the smile fixed on my face and my boobs thrust up. I felt so conspicuous, standing there with my fuck-me clothes on but as well as feeling nervous I felt excited. I could feel the pulse in my pussy as it throbbed inside my thong. My nipples stood out harder than I had ever known and even the feel of the material rubbing against them was like small electric shocks.

I started to look around the room, plenty of potentials. Someone offered to buy me a drink: I didn't like the look of him and told him I was waiting for someone. His eyes lingered on my long legs as he disappointedly moved away. I scanned the room again, who looked like they needed a good fuck … apart from me?

There in the corner was my target. Blond wavy hair and brown eyes, his collar undone and his tie loose, his hands cradled a whisky tumbler. He looked open to persuasion, but more than that he looked hot and by the way he held himself he must work out. I moved up to his table and sat down. My heart began to thump and I tried to steady my breathing.

'Bad day?' I asked, holding onto the table to stop my hands shaking.

'Like you wouldn't believe,' he said, his voice deep and creamy. He tried not to look at my cleavage but couldn't help himself.

'I thought you looked like you needed cheering up.' I leant forward and let him see more of my cleavage.

'Umm yeah.'

'So what is it you do?' I moved my arms together and almost squeezed my tits out of the top of my dress.

'I umm … lecturer.'

'I bet you could teach me a thing or two,' I smiled.

'So … what do you do?' he floundered.

'Oh, you know. Depends on the client.' I held my breath and slipped over one of my cards and as he read it his eyes widened.

'Oh … you're a …'

'That's right.' I slid my foot up his leg. '… and if you want I can be your one.'

He turned red in the face. 'I don't think that …'

'Don't you think I'm sexy?' I moved my hand under the table and ran it up his thigh.

'Oh yes … and getting sexier.'

'Don't you want me?'

'Well … yes … but …'

I moved my hand to his groin, leant forward and whispered in his ear. I could feel him throb through his jeans as I spoke.

'How much?' he asked.

'It has to be cash.' I whispered the price.

'I have it but that seems a lot.'

'Ah but for that I'll also do …' I whispered again and felt his cock try to rip its way out to me. I smiled to myself. Was I really going to do that for him?

Once he had rearranged his hard on so he could walk without getting too much attention we were at the flat. I slammed the door shut so that Mark would know I was here and then led the man to the bedroom shutting the door behind me. He sat on the bed looking as nervous as I felt.

'I haven't been with a … before.'

'Prostitute,' I knew Mark was listening. 'You can call me one it's OK. You're paying you can call me what you like, escort, whore.'

'I haven't been with a prostitute before.'

'All you have to do is enjoy yourself.' No point telling him he was my first as well. I felt my palms go clammy. 'So what do you want?'

'What you said in the pub.'

'That's good. Might as well get your money's worth.'

Temptation got the better of him and he reached out for one of my tits. I pulled away.

'Money first,' I said.

'Oh, of course.'

I knew where the camera had been hidden and turned so that Mark would get to see the transaction. The man took out several notes from his pocket and counted it out into my hand.

'That's perfect,' I said and stuffed the notes into my knicker drawer. Oh my God, I actually took his money, I had sold my body to him and he was going to use it for sex.

'You'd better see what your money gets then.' I stood before him then unzipped the dress and with a wiggle it slid down my legs onto the floor. My bare breasts pushed out brazenly into the air, my nipples throbbing to attention, little islands of dark sticking out from my pale skin. His eyes moved down my flat stomach to the small excuse for underwear that was my thong. I was glad it was black, he wouldn't be able to see the damp patch of anticipation that had spread there; after all, it was him who was supposed to be enjoying it. I felt myself shiver at his gaze and hoped he didn't notice.

He fidgeted on the bed, and his trousers poked out like a tee-pee.

'So do you like what you see?' I asked.

'Oh yes,' he said with his mouth hanging open.

I turned round, 'I've been told I have a sexy arse?'

'You do.'

'I'll just fix my lipstick,' I told him. I faced my dressing table and bent over. I smiled as I heard him gasp. I went through the pretence of doing my lips. I opened my legs slightly and wiggled my arse. I knew he could see my pussy 'mound, the tight material of the thong almost cutting it in two, holding in its juicy soft contents.

I pushed myself right back, and moved to the side a little so that he could see the reflection of my tits swinging in the mirror. His reflection was of wide-eyed wonderment, he seemed to be unsure of what to do next.

'If you want to touch you can,' I invited him closer.

The man stood up and approached me. I was still bending over. His hand tentatively moved out between my legs, his touch no more than a tickle as if daring himself on. I felt his finger trace the line of my crack through the thong; I felt so hot and knew he must feel the same. Then he cupped my pussy with his hand, holding my sex in his palm, I rubbed myself against it and felt my trimmed pubes prickle against him.

'If you want a better look you'd better take my thong off.'

He said nothing, but I could feel his thumbs slide into the thin waistband and pull down. My sticky thong peeled away from my sex and fell down my legs. I took in a sharp breath, I was now fully exposed to him, I didn't even know his name and here I was letting him undress me and stare at my pussy. I thought of Mark watching in the next room and didn't know which was the bigger turn on – having a stranger pay for me, or being watched by my husband. Both were as dirty as each other.

'Did you want to see more?' I asked him and saw his reflection nod.

Still bending over I lifted one foot up onto the chair. My moist lips unfurled and opened for him.

'I'm yours to play with.'

His reply was to slide his hand back between my legs. His fingers running along my slippery crack until they found my hole and then he pushed one inside me. A sigh escaped my lips.

'God you're hot,' he said.

'Hot for a fuck,' I whispered back to him.

He slid another finger into me and it felt divine.

'You're so wet, if I didn't know better I'd say you were enjoying this,' he said.

'I'm just good at my job.' I sighed again as he started to move his fingers in and out.

'Tell me what you want. Let me do the things your girlfriend won't.'

'Well, you could suck it.'

He let his fingers slide from me and I turned around and knelt on the floor in front of him, making sure I was in profile for Mark's camera. Teasingly, I undid his trousers and then pulled his briefs down. His cock sprang out in front of me, swollen and angry, looking big enough to burst. Slowly I began to massage it in my fist, pulling up and down its length, its skin smooth like velvet but the flesh inside as solid as rock

'That's such a big cock. And you want me to put it in my mouth.'

'Yes.'

'Then say it. I want to hear you tell me.' I looked up into his eyes.

'Put my cock in your mouth and suck it.'

I opened wide and guided his pulsing length into me, running it along my tongue as it fitted my mouth. I shut my lips vacuum tight and began to suck. At the same time I kept running my hand up and down him, my other hand fondled his balls, I could feel them full and heavy with come.

His knees buckled slightly as I ran the tip of my tongue around his plum-like knob, pre come smothering it in a salty coat. I swallowed it down. I pushed myself down onto his stalk and then dragged him out of me before sucking him back, and then out, sticky strands still connecting us. His eyes were shut as I hungrily ate his manhood.

'So are you going to come in my mouth or did you want to fuck?' I asked between sucks.

'Fuck,' he said, only half aware of what I was saying.

Leaving my lips glistening and wet I stood up and undid his shirt: his chest was bare and muscular. I ran my nails over it and he shivered. I smiled and led him to the bed. I sat down and then fell back on it opening my legs wide. His gaze fell immediately to my pouting pussy. I obscenely lifted my knees up, I needed something in me so bad I could feel my warm juice drip out.

'Fill me up.'

He didn't need telling twice. He eased himself up me, still wearing his open shirt and then he seemed to hover over me, his cock dripping its eagerness onto my splayed legs. This was it, I thought, as soon as he entered me, I was a prostitute for real, sex for money. A tingle ran down my back, I was nothing but a filthy little pro. I wrapped my legs around his tight arse and pulled him in, thrusting his cock deep into my pussy. I sighed as it burrowed its way in, his large helmet stretching my entrance.

'Talk dirty to me,' he said.

'Doesn't your girlfriend say how she likes to be fucked? How she likes to be stretched by a hard cock ...'

'Keep going.' He started pumping faster, his cock coated in a mixture of our juices.

'Ohh, yes. Stretch my cunt wide open. You're so big.' He started going faster. One of his hands fell to my tits, groping at my flesh.

'Fuck me like the dirty little bitch I am. Ohhh ... that's it ...' He was pushing me through the bed, and it was turning me on so much, firing sparks off in my stomach. I thought I heard a groan from the room opposite, Mark must be having a whale of a time. See if I couldn't make it better for him.

'You know what is a dirty little turn on?'

'What?' he groaned.

'Being taken from behind, I want you to fuck me doggy.' I released him from my legs and flipped over onto my stomach and then, keeping my head on the pillow, I raised my arse high in the air and presented it to him, legs apart. I imagined the sight, red and gaping, and it made me even hotter.

'Fuck me. I need that cock in me now.'

He moved up behind me, grabbed hold of my hips and with a tit-swinging thrust he was inside me. I looked back and could see his balls hanging down between my legs, slapping forwards against my clit.

'That's it, fuck my hole, fuck me hard.' I pushed back onto him to meet his every thrust. 'I want to feel your cock all the way in, grind it into me.'

He started to groan as his cock twitched, he was giving it all he had. My muscles started to give as I felt a wave of energy start to build. 'Oh God, fuck me harder.' His shaft seemed to get bigger and go deeper. I was so hot; pins and needles ran through my pussy and into my stomach. My breathing became a fast panting. Then for a time-stopping moment I climaxed, I yelled out and shivered against him, impaled on length.

My orgasm spurred him on and I could feel he was about to come.

'That's it fuck me like a whore, I'm yours, you paid for me. Fill me with come.'

I kept pushing back onto him and then his body went rigid as he spasmed in my depths, emptying his balls, his spunk overflowing around his cock that still plugged me. He slowed down and then stopped, exhausted he fell out of me and onto the bed.

'You were … fantastic,' he panted.

'Just doing my job,' I smiled back.

I took a minute to get my breath back and then I put on a robe. A few minutes after that the man thanked me and left, looking a lot happier than when I had seen him in the bar. It all seemed too surreal.

Mark came in and looked at me with lust in his eyes.

'Don't bother getting dressed,' he smiled wickedly.

I sat down on the bed and let the robe fall open, 'OK,' I said. 'But payment first and kinks are extra.' After all, a girl has to make a living.